Eddie Black

Eddie Black

a novel by
Walter F. Shapiro

Arbor House / New York

Copyright © 1987 by Walter F. Shapiro

All rights reserved, including the right of reproduction
in whole or in part in any form. Published in the
United States of America by Arbor House Publishing
Company and in Canada by Fitzhenry & Whiteside
Ltd.

Manufactured in the United States of America

10   9   8   7   6   5   4   3   2   1

Library of Congress Cataloging in Publication Data

Shapiro, Walter F.
  Eddie Black.

  I. Title.
PS3569.H34176E3   1987   813'.54   86-17347
ISBN: 0-87795-865-3

Eddie Black

Part One

1

I sat in the truck beside Vincent and watched the women on Seventh Avenue. It was a hot, humid, July afternoon, the only saving grace being it was Friday. The heat made me crazy. I couldn't sleep in it, I couldn't work in it, and I couldn't think in it.

A black girl came out of Village Cigars and stood on the corner. She was wearing a white tank top and white shorts that hugged her behind.

"I have a theory," I said.

"Hit me," said Vincent.

"The sexual drive is all tied up with eating, with hunger. When I see a chick like that I want to grab her, put her on a plate, and bite her ass. I don't mean loving, tender bites, I mean I want to chew the stuff up and digest it. Then I want to eat her pelvis, her legs, her tits, everything. Can you understand that?"

The light changed and he put the truck in gear. "Yeah, I understand it," he said. "I understand you're a sick motherfucker."

"Wrong. I'm in touch with my primitive instincts, that's

all. That's why I'm gonna be a great actor. My agent says I radiate an animal kind of power.''

"Animal kind of bullshit is more like it.''

We were just drifting in the traffic and the black girl was still on the corner. As we drew near I rested my head on my hands by the window and looked her over. Our eyes met for a second and I smiled at her. She looked back at me as if she'd just bit into a lemon.

"I'm not that hard to look at, am I, mama?''

"Shit,'' she said.

"Man,'' said Vincent, "I wish I could rap to women like you do.''

"Hey,'' I said, easing back into the seat. "Even I can't seduce a dyke.''

"Yeah, right, I got it.''

"Are you kidding me? You see the muscles on that chick, the close-cropped hair, that tough man-hating look?''

"Eddie, you shouldn't stereotype people.''

I did a double take and then turned and looked at him. "I shouldn't stereotype people?'' I repeated. "Where the fuck did you get that line?''

He smiled sheepishly. Vincent was about thirty, a couple of years older than me. He had the sort of look you see a lot around New York. Dark features, thick black hair just over the ears, and one of those Fu Manchu mustaches. He was a good guy, and he made this job almost bearable.

"I've decided I'm gonna become more civilized,'' he said. "I'm gonna become a more cultured person.''

"Oh, shit,'' I said. "Let me know when it happens so I can run the other way.'' I banged my fist on the dashboard. "Culture is our worst enemy. It kills everything that's beautiful and strong. If you're not happy with yourself the reason is simple—repression of primitive instincts, and that means fucking and fighting, my man. When was the last time you got into a fistfight?"

"About a year."

"A year? A big healthy male like you should fight at least once a week. When was the last time you saw a nice piece of ass on the street and fucked her where she stood?"

"Come on, man," he said. "You tell me you do that shit?"

"Don't look at me. I'm a coward like everybody else. That's why I'm neurotic. The real heroes in this world are the rapists, the murderers, the people who say fuck the rules, I'm taking what I want, and I'm taking it now. That's what Freud was all about; it just took me to come along and put it into common language."

"I'm sure."

"You're sure. You're developing quite a dry sense of humor. You taking a class at the New School behind my back?"

I stuck my head out the window and took a deep breath. I can't do this job anymore, I thought. It's making me crazy. I'd been working at Popowski's Meats for almost six months. It was hard, dull work, but it paid almost five hundred dollars a week in cash, which was nice because I was still collecting unemployment. I was going to quit at the end of the summer and start going to auditions again. I'd been acting on and off for about seven years, and didn't have much to show for it yet; some small theatre, two walk-on film parts, and a couple of commercials, but my break wasn't going to come in this meat truck.

We were under the West Side Highway, and Vincent pulled off into the gravel lot by the river where we kept the truck. We locked up and started back to the office.

"You really believe that stuff you said about culture?" he asked.

"I don't know," I said tiredly. "I was just talking."

He started to say something, hesitated, and then spoke in a voice that quivered slightly. "Julie's been putting a lot of pressure on me to go back to school and to read books and shit like that. She's studying art history, and she says she's growing."

I glanced at him. He was walking woodenly with his eyes downward, staring at the gravel.

"Are you interested in doing those things?" I asked him.

"I don't know. I tried, but I don't know. I tried to read this book . . . *Madame Bovary.* I got about five pages into it; I had to put it away and turn on the stereo."

I smiled. "Yeah, I didn't like it either."

"You didn't?"

"No, I thought it was boring."

"When I say that, Julie says I'm ignorant."

Our pace had already slowed to a crawl, and I stopped and faced him. "Sounds like you got a problem."

"She wants to leave me," he said, his voice cracking. "She's all I got, man."

At that moment one of the other trucks owned by our company pulled up near us. The driver, a pimply-faced kid named Mickey, stuck his head out the window. "You faggots want a ride back to the shop?"

Vincent didn't budge. I spoke to Mickey. "We'll be along in a minute." I turned back to Vincent. "That's not true. She's one woman, one human being. She's not all you got."

He looked hard at me. His eyes were moist, but they were also angry. "She's making a big mistake, I'll tell you that," he said, his voice rising frantically. "She will never ever find another guy that will love her like I do. And after all the bullshit is said and done the bottom line is still love. Am I right?"

I didn't answer.

"Am I right?"

"I don't know."

"Is that all you got to say?" He stepped forward and grabbed me by the T-shirt, scratching my neck. I swung my arms up, breaking his grip on me, and then I pushed him backward. Our eyes locked and for a moment I was sure he was going to come at me, but a second later the tension broke and both our bodies relaxed in one shudder. He walked up to me and put his hand on my elbow. "It's the heat, man," he said. "Let's get the fuck out of here."

Frank Popowski stood in the center of the loading dock with his arms folded as we approached the office. He was in his late fifties, bald, and built like a fire hydrant. Despite the heat he was dressed as always—the blood-smeared butcher's smock buttoned all the way to the top and a Mets baseball cap worn backward. As we drew near I could see the scowl on his face and I braced myself. Frank had two basic moods— gruff and nasty.

"You didn't get the check at Hoffman's," he said to me.

All business, I reached into my back pocket and pulled out a sheaf of receipts. I rifled through them quickly and held one of them out to him. "It's not in the papers. It doesn't say to pick up a check."

He slapped at the receipt in disgust, ripping it almost completely in half. "I gotta spell everything out for you jerks? The guy pays on Friday. I gotta put a full-page ad in *The New York Times*?"

"Oh, fuck you!" I shot back. "You're the one always

crying about following instructions and doing the paperwork. You fucked up. Don't blame us."

"I want that check today."

"Come on, Frank," I said more softly. "What's the big deal? We'll get it on Monday."

"Bullshit. I don't trust that Jew over the weekend."

Vincent stepped forward. "Hey, don't you know Eddie's Jewish?"

"Yeah, like I know you're a Wop. And neither one of youse is worth shit."

I tried to reason with him. "Frank, we made twenty-seven stops today. We're not bookkeepers. You always put it on the papers. You forgot, admit it."

"I ain't admitting nothin'. You can talk all you want. I got your pay inside. You guys want your money, you go up to Hoffman's and get the check. He's there 'til six." With that, Frank turned on his heel and stamped into the office.

Vincent and I cursed into the air for a couple of minutes and then sat on the loading dock. Vincent was talking to himself under his breath. He kept saying, "It ain't right," over and over again.

The street was completely deserted. The only movement at all was the slow trickle of cars moving up Hudson Street to our left. But our block was warehouses and a few loft dwellers, and there was nobody around. Even Schwartz, the egg man, who seemed built into his building across the street and worked until seven every night, had closed down.

I wondered if there was some great sin I was trying to atone for. There were men this moment, and I could see them vividly, lying on beaches in the Hamptons. Soon they'd drive home, shower, and dress in whites. They would go out and eat crabmeat salads, drink gin and tonics, and fuck well-bred women. They'd sleep in air-conditioning. My life is much more authentic, I thought drily. I sit here in ninety-seven degrees of pollution, exhausted to the point of delirium, to be bled to death by a crazy Polack butcher.

I sure as hell wasn't going back up to Hoffman's for that check. It would probably mean my job, but I knew I was through with this anyway—it was bad for me. It wasn't the physical work or the driving around in the truck, but the constant proximity to raw, bloody meat. It had done something to me. I was beginning to develop a crude, almost bestial mentality. At first I had liked it, but enough was enough. For the first time in my life I had a few grand in the bank, a little less than I'd wanted to have before leaving, but it would have to do.

I looked over at Vincent. He seemed to be doing some calculations of his own.

"What do you want to do?" I said.

"I want my money," he said grimly.

"Let's get it."

We went inside. Frank was sitting behind the meat counter in his beat-up swivel chair. His back was to us as he leaned over the desk doing paperwork. He acknowledged our presence by holding up his left hand and giving us the finger.

I tried to speak with calmness and strength. "We're here for our money, Frank."

"You got the check?" he asked, still not turning around.

"No."

He got out of the chair slowly, hitched up his pants, and faced us over the counter. "If you don't get the check, you're fired."

"Fine."

"Great," said Vincent.

Frank's face darkened. He actually looked hurt for a second. "Okay, you're all through. Come by late next week for your money. In the meantime, get lost—you no-good fucks."

He sat down in his chair and turned back to the desk. Vincent strode around the counter and with a vicious upward motion of his hand he knocked the Mets cap off of Frank's head. Frank roared and started to rise from his chair, but Vincent caught him with a straight right to the chin. The punch knocked Frank directly back into the chair, and its momentum toppled both him and the chair backward into a heap on the floor. Vincent was on top of him immediately, slapping him across the face and screaming obscenities. I had leaned over the counter and was watching them, with my chin resting on my hands.

Finally Frank managed to speak hoarsely. "Okay, let me up. I'll pay youse now."

Vincent stopped, but looked genuinely torn between hitting Frank some more or getting the money. I yelled, "Let him up!"

Frank got to his feet huffing and puffing. "You fucking bastard," I said to him.

He smoothed out his butcher's coat absurdly, as if it was a nice suit, and then without looking at either of us he went into the back room to get the money.

Vincent and I nodded grimly to each other as we waited.

Frank reappeared. His face and head were beet red and he still breathed heavily. In his left hand he held a cigar box. In his right was a huge carving knife. He held the knife firmly near his waist, the blade pointed at Vincent's gut. He placed the cigar box on the shelf behind him and spoke to Vincent. "Come and get your money, you fucking Dago."

Vincent didn't move. His mouth was open, his eyes alert, almost playful. He had his knees slightly bent and bounced slowly on the balls of his feet. His hands were up around his chest and out in front of him.

Frank smiled maliciously and moved forward. He said something and Vincent backed up. My body was nailed to the floor, but I could hear myself yelling at Frank to stop and Vincent to run.

Vincent was no more than five feet from the wall now, and Frank was yelling something at him which I couldn't make out; the words came to me in primitive sounds.

I was still yelling too, but the sound of my own voice was negligible. It had just blended into the scene. My body trembled to a nearly unbearable rhythm as I inched my way around the counter.

I was about to hurl myself onto Frank's shoulders when my eye caught sight of one of the smaller carving knives on the cutting table, not six inches from my left hand. A sick, vacant sensation rose in my stomach and went straight to my head. The knife seemed to disappear and then appear again. It changed sizes; it moved around. In my hand, it sloshed around in the sweat, so I had to hold it as tight as I could to hold it at all.

"Frank!" I yelled at the top of my lungs, though I wasn't sure if anything came out. He was oblivious to me anyway and kept moving forward—a fat, bald machine. "Stop!" I yelled again. This time my voice was clear and powerful, and it rendered mute all other sound in the room. And this time he stopped; the blade of my knife was buried in the middle of his back.

I looked across at Vincent. He seemed a long way off, and I could barely make out his features. His eyes met mine for a second, and then he turned into a mass of activity. I saw him lean over Frank and then turn toward the sink and turn the water on. He went into the back room for a minute, and

when he returned he opened the cigar box and took all the
money that was in it.

"What are you doing?" I whispered.

He came over to me and grabbed me by the shoulders.
"Listen to me. Frank got held up. When he tried to fight back
they killed him. That's what happened."

I tried to focus on his face and started to shake my head,
but he squeezed me tighter. "You want to go to jail for this
scum? You want to be in prison for ten years?"

"They'll find out," I breathed.

"They ain't gonna find out shit!" he said harshly. "I
washed out the knife, there's nobody around," he gestured
around the room. "This is a robbery, man. We take our pay
out of here—I'll ditch the rest and we split. The cops call and
you don't know nothing. You're smart, don't be stupid. In
your left nut you're worth ten of that motherfucker. Just listen to me."

I did. Ten minutes later I, Eddie Black, day laborer,
sometime actor, and killer, was on the Lexington Avenue
Local with my money in my pocket. Another working stiff
going home for the weekend. Except I didn't feel like a stiff. I
wasn't even tired anymore.

2

The only light was the glow of my cigarette, and the only motion was my right hand as it controlled the cigarette and my left as it occasionally lifted the bottle of bourbon to my lips.

I was sitting on the couch, naked, in the breathless night. I held my left hand out in front of me. In the dark, it was perfectly still, though it did seem to change shapes and go through transformations as objects sometimes will when stared at. Every few minutes an image of the knife on the table appeared before me, and I felt the same empty sickness wash through my body, but each time it passed.

Mostly, my mind wandered in unlikely directions: when I was eleven years old and walking through a country trail upstate, on my way to play baseball. I remembered staring at a tuft of grass and wondering dimly if this moment could be different from all the other moments in my life that already seemed lost and meaningless. Now, thinking of it, I could see the exact formation of the ground, smell the vegetation and the dust, and I could even sense the excitement of being that young, lean, and quick in my shorts and Keds, and going to play baseball.

There was Ellen: the first to give me sexual pleasure
and the exquisite gift of her touch. Also, the first female I'd
ever been able to talk to. At thirteen we had decided, in complete seriousness, that come what may, when we were both
twenty-one we would meet on the steps of the New York
Public Library and look back on our lives and share all the
wisdom we had acquired. We had even set a date for it; and
the knowledge that that day had come and gone without a
thought from either of us made me sad.

The phone rang. This was the second time. I'd let the
first one go seven times before it stopped, and this one also
rang exactly seven. I began to mentally tick off a list of plau-
sible callers, but the possibilities seemed endless and unin-
teresting.

I ran my hand along the bottom of my cock, and a bead
of sweat formed on my right temple. I put out the cigarette,
swung my legs up on the couch, and masturbated. I came
powerfully and then lay still as the drone of the refrigerator
filled the apartment. It got louder and louder, bouncing off
the walls and hammering my eardrums. This must be the
end, I thought gratefully, for I was ready; and then it stopped.

An hour later I was sitting in a small bar a few blocks
from the apartment. I ordered a shot of Bushmills, another
one, and a third. I could sense the place filling up, but I
didn't look around. My world consisted of the bartender, my
shot glass, the palpable weight of my thoughts, and no more.

After a while I began to relax. This was from the liquor,
but also from the proximity to people. People is what it's all
about, I thought sentimentally. From now on I will pursue
people, not abstract ideas like fulfillment and fame and sex. A
damn good resolution, I told myself, and clever too.

"Can you pass the ashtray please?" The voice came
from my immediate left, and it belonged to a woman in

her middle twenties with dark wavy hair and large brown eyes. She was unusually pretty, but I noted it dispassionately. She belonged to the living world of movement and relation, and I belonged to something else. I slid the ashtray between us.

But the exchange had broken my reverie, and I found myself eavesdropping on her conversation. She was with a guy, but I could tell from the dialogue they didn't know each other. He was a plump, balding man of about forty with a friendly, I-aim-to-please sort of face. He wore glasses and a cheap rumpled suit. It wasn't really a conversation I was listening to because he was doing all the talking, chattering on about his job and the people he worked with as if it was all headline news. There was a desperateness about him like a vapor; you could smell it.

A heavy-set girl with a lot of makeup appeared between us and got a light off me. When she left, the one at the bar said, "I wonder why she asked you and not me?"

"I don't know," I replied. "Maybe she could see you were busy."

She smiled at me with her eyes, which were really fine, and said, "A fool could see I'm not busy."

I sipped on my drink and a minute later she spoke to me again. "I know who you are, you know."

A quick rush of anxiety ran through my chest, but when I looked at her I immediately relaxed. "Do you mean that in some ultimate sense?" I asked.

She laughed and shook her head. "I saw you in a television commercial a few years ago, but that's not where I really know you from. I went to Harbor Hill. You played basketball for Chesley Academy."

"Chesley Academy?" I repeated, with surprise. "You have some memory."

She shrugged. "I was friendly with the coach at Harbor Hill. He used to stay up nights devising ways to stop you from shooting. A Jewish Jerry West, that's what he called you."

It felt unnatural, almost painful to laugh. "No shit," I said. "I kind of like that. It has a certain ring to it."

"Didn't you get a scholarship somewhere?"

"Yeah, but it didn't work out."

"Why not?"

"Well, it came down to a decision. Either I could play basketball or shoot dope. I chose the road more easily traveled."

She looked at me seriously and nodded.

"Anyway," I said, keeping my tone light, "I took a few years off, got it together a little, and went to drama school."

"Hmm, that's interesting."

"It's fascinating." I turned my body toward her, and the deep, rich, nearly sweet odor of her floated into my nostrils. "So," I said. "What else did you and the coach do at night besides worry about the Jewish Jerry West?"

"I was fourteen years old," she replied. "He was my first."

I murmured in a tone of respect, "Was it poignant?"

She looked at me wistfully for a moment before answering. "No. I guess it should have been, but it wasn't."

"Too bad."

She smiled to herself and said, "Can I make a confession?"

"Sure."

"I used to stare at you during the games. I used to watch your skinny belly and legs. I would fantasize sometimes . . ." She dropped her eyes demurely and said, "I don't want to talk about this."

"Oh, come on. Let's hear the fantasy."

She waved me off with her hand. "I shouldn't have even brought it up, it's too crazy. I'm a writer, sort of. I'm still finding my style, and I've been thinking about language a lot, you know, how words are mostly used to hide things. I haven't figured it out yet, but I think I'm just experimenting with an intense sort of bluntness. You know what I mean? Does that make any sense?"

"Sure. Now tell me what you fantasized."

"I couldn't."

I turned away from her and picked up my drink. "The experiment with bluntness is a failure," I said.

"What do you mean?"

"What I mean is that it's easy to be abstract, but it's the concrete that's important. That's the way it is with acting, and that's the way it must be with writing."

"That's true," she said, smiling broadly. "But you have to have some regard for the person on the other end, and I don't think you'd understand."

"Oh, come on," I said. "I've read Freud, Reich, all them guys. I've dressed in women's clothing. You can trust me."

She looked at me seriously and bit her lip. "I fantasized throwing you on a table and eating you piece by piece."

"Piece by piece?"

"Your balls were on top, as a sort of dressing, as a spice. Your ass was the main course."

"What about my cock?"

"It was on the side, like a pickle."

I nodded in an almost professional manner and looked at her. She was smiling nervously, and there was a hint of a challenge in her expression.

"I do have a question," I said.

"What's that?"

"This pickle. Was it a skinny slice like you get in a coffee shop with a hamburger, or was it like a whole dill pickle that you buy in a deli?"

She started laughing, first with her eyes, then in short low sounds, and finally in a girlish sort of giggle.

The guy next to her leaned over and said, "This a private party?"

She glanced at him quickly, as if he was a mosquito or something, and said, "Yes, it is."

I felt a mild stab of pain for the guy. Only a woman, I thought, could be so casually cold.

She put her chin on her upturned hand and looked at me dreamily. "I want to hear one of your fantasies."

"I'm having one right now," I said, wiping my mouth with the back of my hand, a gesture I didn't remember ever having made before. "Want me to relate it?"

"Yes, please relate it."

"Okay. You're lying naked on my bed, spread-eagled. I have your buttocks in my hands, and my face between your legs. Needless to say, you're quite wet . . ."

"Needless to say."

"Yeah, and I'm really working out. I'm hungry for you. and you taste so sweet that I can't get enough. You're moaning and then screaming—a lot of Biblical names." I hesitated. "This isn't all that original, is it?"

"Oh, don't stop now," she said. "You're doing so well."

"Anyway, you come in a giant crescendo amid paroxysms of pleasure and slump on the bed, unconscious."

"Unconscious?"

"Yeah."

"Do I wake up?"

"Yes. And you're ravenous. You catch me in the bathroom, drag me back to bed, and start screwing me from on top. Your hips are marvelous, your movements are wild, but graceful. I reach a state where the pleasure is so intense it becomes painful, but I go beyond that, and just when I'm about to come a figure appears before my eyes, on the ceiling. It's an old white man with a beard. His face is wrinkled, but his eyes are all the colors of the rainbow, and so bright that they light up the room. It's God. I finally find Him, or He finds me. Whatever."

"Does He say anything?"

"Yes," I replied soberly. "He says, 'here is your choice, little man. You can either exhaust your pettiness into this woman, or you can fly with me to the mountain tops. The air is cold and raw there, but you can see forever.' " I paused and took a swig of liquor.

"What did you do?" she asked urgently.

"I gave him the finger, and took my pleasure."

She stared into my eyes for a couple of seconds and then turned away. I ordered another drink and lighted a cigarette. When I looked at her again she was leaning forward with her head in her hands. She was wearing faded blue jeans, and I took a moment to look at the configuration of her ass and legs where they met the bar stool. I nudged her elbow with mine, and said, "What's your name?"

She turned and faced me. Her eyes were moist and luminous. She was either deeply sad, deeply happy, or both. I saw myself lean over and kiss her on the lips, but I didn't do it. "My name is Charlotte," she said slowly, "and I want you to take me to a Chinese restaurant."

I smiled and was about to tell her what an inspired idea that was when I felt a hand grip my arm. I turned around to look into the face of Mickey, the kid from work. Before I could even begin to assimilate his presence here he said, "Eddie!"

"Mickey . . ."

"I been trying to reach you," he snapped, giving Charlotte the once over. "You hear about Frank?"

I stared at him, my heart pounding.

"He's dead. A holdup right in the shop. They stabbed him to death."

I closed my eyes and shook my head. "No, it can't be."

"Yes," said Mickey excitedly. "They hit him right after work, right after you and Vinny left, I guess. I been telling him for two years not to leave so much cash around."

Charlotte was holding my wrist, and it was the only thing preventing a total breakdown on my part.

"My cousin's a cop," continued Mickey. "He works that precinct. He called me up and told me all about it."

"Oh, God," I said.

"Yeah," he said. "It's heavy. Frank could be a prick, but he was good people. And I'll tell you another thing. All our asses are out of a job, and forget about unemployment. We ain't even on the books."

I pulled my arm free of Charlotte and brushed past Mickey. Once outside, I knelt between two parked cars and alternately vomited and gagged for what seemed like a long time.

It was raining now, not hard, but in a fine mist. I stood up and leaned on one of the cars. I took deep breaths, and the pores of my skin sucked up the moisture.

The door to the bar opened, and Charlotte appeared outside of it. She made no move toward me, but none to leave either. My eyes rested on the outline of her breasts against the blue T-shirt. I knew it must be warm there, and suddenly I was so cold. I took a step toward her and smiled inwardly. I didn't feel really so bad. Perhaps I have already seen the devil, and he is mine. My second step was more difficult, and it seemed as if I was moving in slow motion as I watched my foot go down toward the ground. When will it get there? I wondered. And that was my last thought before blacking out. I pitched forward and down to the pavement, as Charlotte told me later, like a dead man.

The next thing I knew I was sitting on the curb, and she was next to me, her hand under my chin, and her eyes searching mine. I became aware of some other people around, and when I looked at them I saw fear in their eyes. But Charlotte was completely calm and in control. I don't remember what she was saying, but she kept using my name, and I really liked the way it sounded on her lips.

3

"**Y**ou look strange," said Charlotte. "Don't you like it here?"

It was Sunday morning, and we were sitting at the kitchen table of her parents' house in Vermont. Charlotte was wearing a brown silk bathrobe; the color matched her eyes.

"I like it fine," I replied. "I was just thinking it's been three years since I've been out of the city. I'm just getting used to the silence. And those mountains. They have a name, don't they?"

"Yeah, they're the Green Mountains. Vermont is the Green Mountain State."

Charlotte had picked me up on Saturday around dinnertime and we'd driven up in her Datsun, arriving near midnight. Her parents lived in Connecticut and used this place for weekends and vacations, but they weren't around right now. It was nice: five bedrooms on a lot of land and from where I was sitting at the table all I could see was the long green expanse of the backyard, and the mountains.

We hadn't exactly traded life stories, but I knew something about her now. She had just returned from two years in Asia where, as part of some philanthropic organization, she had worked in settlements for the poor and refugee camps. I thought that was pretty interesting, but Charlotte was distinctly reticent on the matter, saying only that the experience had all but convinced her that there was no political hope for mankind. Shit, I could've told her that and saved her a trip.

She was living in the city now, in the West Village, and taking a shot at writing. I read some of her stuff on the way up, a short story about sexual tension between two women. It was an allusive, impressionistic piece, of the type which usually give me a headache, but I liked it. She had her own way of writing, and the story was powerful enough that I kept thinking about it.

Charlotte was more interested in hearing about me than she was in talking about herself, and I found myself expansive in her presence. I talked about my difficulties with acting in a much more personal way than I was accustomed to, and when I told her I'd been married and had a seven-year-old son she really lit up, and I got off on a string of anecdotes about my kid, Benjamin.

A strange thing happened as I spoke to her. Charlotte seemed to think it was all fascinating and wonderful. Through her eyes my life took on a dynamic quality. She transmitted to me a sense of possibility, and by the end of the ride I was indulging in all manner of optimisms. After all, I was twenty-eight years old, strong and healthy; I could think, I could fuck, and I had problems that were worthy of me.

Now, she led me outside, onto a wooden terrace off the kitchen. We sat in folding chairs, and I filled my lungs with the good air.

"I said I loved you last night," she said quietly.

I turned and looked at her. She was staring out at the mountains with her body hunched down in the chair and her long legs carelessly splayed out on the deck.

"Are you sorry?" I asked.

"Maybe."

"Don't be sorry," I said softly. "It sounded good to me. And besides, I won't hold you to it."

She looked at me quizzically. "What do you mean?"

"We were in bed. It was a nice thing to say."

I saw a wave of anger pass through her and disappear. She got out of her chair and walked over to the edge of the terrace. She spoke deliberately, throwing her voice out toward the mountains. "Thank you, Eddie, that's very considerate of you."

I watched her lean on the railing and felt bad for having hurt her. I hadn't meant to. I went over and pressed my body lightly against hers. I kissed her neck, her shoulders, and through the robe I caressed her body with my hands. When I turned her around I could feel the heat coming off of her, and with a flick of my finger I opened the robe and we came together in a long, Hollywood-style embrace. A minute later I was inside her, her bottom resting on my hands. Charlotte's eyes were half closed and swimming in liquid. I kissed her softly and put my mouth to her ear.

"You're so fine," I whispered.

I pressed her more firmly against me, rotating her behind in a sideways circular motion as she clung to me. My legs and arms were like rocks, oblivious to the strain of Charlotte's body, and when she was done she couldn't stand, but gently crumpled onto the deck of the terrace.

I stood in the middle of the terrace, my cock still hard, and stared at the great Green Mountains. I felt equal to them, I felt like some kind of god.

I glanced at Charlotte. She was staring up at me curiously, almost smiling. She had caught me in my pretension, and we both laughed.

She half crawled, half slid, to where I was standing and took me in her hand. "Looks like you still have a problem," she said.

"Yes," I whispered. "Do you know a cure?"

"Well," she said, giving the tip of me a small wet kiss, "there is always a cold shower."

I moaned softly and then I reached down and touched the side of her head. "What else?"

Later we were lying on a big rock above a quarry near the house. The quarry itself was about the size of a football field, and there were eight or ten other people scattered about on different rocks.

"Does this happen to you often?" she asked.

"What?"

"Pick up some woman on Friday night—spend the weekend with her."

"You picked me up."

"I did not," she said quickly. And then, "What if I did? You think I'm a bad girl?"

"Yeah. It's the only kind of girl I like."

She stood up and executed a perfect dive into the water. She swam the length of it and back. I watched her long graceful body as she climbed back toward me.

"You're beautiful," I said to her.

Pretending not to hear, she sat down with her knees bent and started to comb out her hair. "I wish we could go away someplace for a while."

"We already are away someplace."

"No, I mean far away, like Paris or Venice or even San Francisco."

I sighed and lay down, closing my eyes to the sun.

"I gather the idea doesn't appeal to you."

"Traveling is for fools," I replied.

"For fools? Who told you that?"

"No one told me. But I see tourists around New York all the time, and they make me sick. People that live in Paris or Venice or San Francisco should be allowed to live there in peace without assholes in Bermuda shorts and dumb smiles walking around taking pictures of everything."

She giggled and said, "I can't see you in Bermuda shorts."

"And you won't."

She stopped combing her hair and looked at me. "If you don't like traveling, what do you like?"

I sat up halfway and leaned on my elbows. Across the water two women in their forties had arrived with children, and I watched them take their clothes off. "I like acting, I guess."

She murmured with satisfaction. "When did you decide that?"

"I don't know when I decided it first, but I remember in my first year of drama school we did a scene in class from *Othello*. I played Othello, and it was the scene where he kills Desdemona. Something happened for me then. I was transported into the role, I mean really transported. When the scene was over and I looked up, it was as if I had just come back from a voyage to a distant planet where all the rules were mine. It was mystical. I knew I had to have that sensation back, again and again."

"And have you?"

"No. I'm beginning to think it was an acid flashback or some quirk like that."

"You shouldn't think that way. You shouldn't denigrate it like that."

I smiled and lay back down. "Yeah, you're right."

"When I was in college," she said, "I wrote a story that was read in class. It wasn't exactly great literature; I mean, I read it now and it makes me cringe. But it had a lot of emotion, and some of it must have gotten through because some of the people in class were actually crying. I remember looking around the room as it was being read—I was intoxicated. I decided then that that was the only kind of power worth having, and I wanted more of it."

"Have you gotten more of it?"

"I dunno. Here and there. I'm still working on it."

I moved my foot slightly so that it touched hers, and we didn't speak for a few minutes.

"Charlotte, I said I loved you this morning."

"Yeah," she replied, "but you were in an excited state. I didn't take it seriously."

I laughed and glanced over at her. She was smiling sadly. She leaned over me, putting her cigarette on the rock between my legs. She kissed me on the lips and rested her head on my chest. The cigarette hadn't completely burned out yet, and we lay there watching the smoke rise upward. It looked as if it was coming from my penis.

"Hot stuff," said Charlotte.

"You better believe it," I said.

After dinner I went downstairs to the den and dialed Vincent's number in Brooklyn. As the phone rang my heart began to pound. What if he wasn't there? A scenario emerged in my mind: We had left some obvious piece of evidence and the cops had already picked Vincent up. My picture was plastered all over the newspapers, and Frank's family had posted a reward for my capture . . .

"Hullo," mumbled Vincent, his voice full of sleep.

"Vincent!"

There was a pause. "Eddie?"

"Yeah."

"Jesus, man, where are you?"

"I'm out of town," I replied. "I went away for a few days."

"I got worried," he said. "I thought you just freaked out and split. That would've been a disaster."

"No. I'm here. I'm coming home tomorrow. Anything happening?"

"Not really," he said. "The cops came by here yesterday."

"Are you shitting me?"

"Relax," he said. "Just routine questions. Did he have any enemies? Did I see anyone around the shop, that kind of stuff."

"What'd you tell them?"

Vincent grunted ironically. "What do you think I told them? I told them shit. I told them less than shit."

I leaned back in the big leather chair and took a deep breath. I felt a hollow kind of fear in my chest, and though it was cool down here, my body was sticky with sweat. The room was obviously designed for comfort, relaxation, and even reflection. Most of the other furniture was also leather, and very comfortable. Directly in front of me was a marble fireplace flanked by two floor-to-ceiling bookcases. The carpeting was a thick, soft brown—the whole room in fact was done in soft browns and beige. In the corner was a beautiful antique rolltop desk and chair. I tried to imagine Charlotte's father—she'd said he was an investment banker—sitting right there where I was and pondering (probably in satisfaction) his various contributions to the world.

"Vincent, you remember Angelina's?"

"What? The restaurant?"

"Yeah, the one we used to deliver to."

"Sure."

"Ever take a piss there?"

"In the bathroom?"

I hesitated, glancing at the receiver. "No, in the manicotti. Of course in the bathroom."

"Sure."

"You remember there used to be a piece of graffiti on the wall just above the urinal? It said, 'It's all a dream.' Remember that?"

"Yeah, I think I remember it. It sounds familiar. Stupid, but familiar."

"You thought it was stupid?"

"Very."

"I thought it was brilliant. I thought it was profound."

"That's cool," replied Vincent. "It hit you one way, it hit me the other."

"Sometimes I feel like what happened to Frank is a dream."

He laughed without humor. "Ain't no dream, Eddie. The man's dead."

"Vincent, do you feel any guilt about this?"

"Guilt?" He repeated the word as if he'd never heard it before. "What does guilt have to do with it? It was a bad thing, it happened. It was more his fault than anybody else's. You don't feel guilty about it, do you?"

"No," I replied. "I keep looking around for it, but it's not there. I think I feel guilty about not feeling guilty."

"Are you dropping acid up there?"

"Maybe we should get a good lawyer and confess."

Even over the telephone Vincent's silence was palpably ominous. "What did you say?" he asked.

I took a deep breath. "You heard what I said. It's just a thought."

"It's a bad thought," he replied. "It's the worst thought you ever had."

"Take it easy. I just think it's a good idea to look at options."

"We only have two options," he said. "It's either freedom or a whole lot of hard time."

"I hear about people walking free for all kinds of stuff."

"Oh, man," said Vincent disgustedly, "what you're talking about is fourteen-year-old niggers and psychos. Eddie, if we go up for this it's twenty-five to life. Think about twenty-five to life."

"Okay," I said. "What are these cops like?"

"No problem," said Vincent. "The head guy is one of your people—name is Greenberg, Nate Greenberg. A little bit of a wise guy, but you can handle him easy. Just keep it simple."

"A Jewish detective?" I said. "I thought they were all Irish."

"What the fuck is the difference?" he said impatiently.

"I don't know. I don't want to think about it."

"That's the best idea I've heard yet. You think too much, Eddie, and it worries me. It's your, what do you call it, we talked about it in the truck one day, something about a heel."

"Achilles' heel."

"Yeah, Achilles' heel. All you gotta think about is the story. We came back on Friday afternoon, he paid us, and we split. Capishe?"

"Okay."

Vincent's equanimity was contagious, and I was starting to feel a lot calmer.

"By the way," he said, "where are you?"

"I'm in Vermont."

"Not bad," said Vincent. "I didn't know you had a country place."

"No," I replied. "I met a lady. It's unbelievable."

"Nice place, huh?"

"No, I mean the girl."

"Oh, shit," he said, "you're too much." And then, more quietly, "You didn't tell her anything, did you?"

"Vincent, you really don't trust me, do you?"

"There is no such thing," he replied, as if reading from a book, "as absolute trust. Eddie Black, nineteen eighty."

He was right. I'd forgotten the circumstance, but I remembered saying it. Now there was an uncomfortable tension between us, but I could think of nothing to say that would dispel it.

"Speaking of Achilles' heels," I said finally, "what's with Julie?"

"She moved out last night. It's over."

"I'm sorry."

"Me too."

I was lying in bed next to Charlotte, considering the prospect of returning to New York in the morning. I had plenty to think about, but mostly I thought about her. What would it be like seeing her in the city?

I didn't know much about her or the way she lived. She could have someone else; she might be inclined to just end this now; a small piece of lusty perfection. She wrote short stories, so that would figure. Also, I had noticed in her a mysterious preoccupation at times. She would be thinking intensely with her brow furrowed and then glance at me quickly, as if wondering if I could be trusted. I thought of Vincent and smiled sadly: "There is no such thing as absolute trust."

"What are you thinking about?" she asked softly.

"I'm thinking about us," I replied, emphasizing the last word for relief.

She took a deep breath and said, "That's a biggie."

"Is it?"

She didn't answer, and finally I turned my head to look at her and saw the stream of tears running down her face. I nudged her. "Hey, nothing's that serious."

She turned toward me, and I had to smile. She looked like a child, with her lips puffed out, her red eyes, and her pouting expression. She saw me smile, and that stopped her crying for the moment. She grabbed some tissues by the night table and started to clean herself up. "Eddie," she started, but her voice cracked and she really broke down this time, sobbing loudly. I couldn't help but recall the innumerable scenes much like this during my marriage to Laura. And it made me cringe when I thought of how stupid I'd been then, never understanding, always demanding rational, on-the-spot explanations for her tears.

After a while, Charlotte stopped and went into the bathroom. She returned dry-faced, composed, and looking a little older. I was struck by her beauty. It was of the kind people sometimes attain when utterly lost—a simple and unadorned humanity. She sat in a chair at the far end of the room and lighted a cigarette. "I'm confused," she said.

Her eyes didn't really focus on me; they swallowed me up. There was something so powerful in her gaze that it made me feel very small. "There's someone else," she said quietly.

I leaned back on the pillow and closed my eyes. Much as I'd tried to anticipate something like this, I was devastated. Charlotte started to speak, and had I possessed the strength I would have stopped her because I really didn't want to hear it.

"I fell in love with my history professor in college," she said, "and we went to Asia together after I graduated."

"That's nice," I said glumly.

"And now we live together."

"Well, great," I said, raising my head off the pillow. "I hope you live happily ever after, you and . . . what's his name?"

"Margaret."

I stared at her hard. There was a smile playing in her eyes, but she wasn't kidding. "Oh, shit," I said, and I rolled over on my stomach. Charlotte came over and watched me, smiling curiously.

"Eddie, does it upset you more or less because it's a woman?"

It upset me a lot less. I was even beginning to find it funny, but I wasn't about to tell her that. "What is this?" I asked. "A survey?"

She started to stroke my back, and we didn't speak for a minute or two. "Charlotte," I said, "how is it being with me?"

"Dangerous," she replied without hesitation.

"Is that good?"

She took a deep breath. "Probably. The sex is powerful; it scares me. When we're not doing it I'm thinking about it. I never felt that way before."

"Does Margaret know we're together?"

She shrugged absently. "I'm supposed to be up here writing. But that's not really the point. If she knew she'd probably be amused."

"Amused?"

"Yeah. I've been off men for a while. I reached a point where even the thought of going to bed with a man repulsed me. But there was something about the way you looked in the bar; it wasn't even primarily sexual, it was some kind of energy that I couldn't figure out."

"Don't forget," I said playfully, "you had a crush on me in high school."

"Oh, that's right!" she said, laughing. "I almost forgot." She became serious again. "Eddie, does it bother you?"

"Does what bother me?"

"To know you've been sleeping with a dyke. I expected you to come unglued."

I turned over onto my back so we were facing each other. I stroked the side of her face and looked into her eyes.

"If only that were my biggest problem."

Part Two

4

I got home on Monday night at around eight. After the big house and the open spaces in Vermont, my studio apartment felt like a dollhouse, and I found myself moving about carefully to avoid bumping into the furniture. I poured myself a drink, sat on the couch, and flicked on the answering machine. A few clicks and then a female voice. "Edward," she said, "this is your mother." Pause for effect. "If I should drop dead you would be the last to know. Call me. I want you to come to dinner, and I want to see my grandson."

Two more clicks and then Laura. I silently hummed the words, "the women in my life," to no tune at all. "Eddie . . . hi. It's Laura." Pause for effect. "Benjamin's been asking for you. God, I hate these machines. I don't know what your schedule is like these days, I've been trying to reach you all weekend. I don't know if you're away, or what, but uh . . ." I smiled to myself. Wouldn't you like to know? "If you can find time to call, then maybe we can arrange something."

Next came a deep, gravelly voice. "Uh, Edward Black. This is Detective Greenberg of the New York City Police De-

37

partment. I want to ask you a couple of questions about
Frank Popowski. I'd appreciate a call at 999-4400 between
the hours of nine and five, and if I'm not there leave a message.''

I sat unmoving as he spoke, and then I replayed the
message twice, laboring over each word for any hidden attitude or meaning. I turned the machine off and lighted a cigarette. Nothing to worry about, I concluded finally. Greenberg
sounded like a bored bureaucrat going through the motions.

The next voice on the machine was a complete surprise.
Dolores Barnes was a middle-aged Jewish lady from Queens,
but she spoke with a British accent. "Eddie, this is Dolores
Barnes, your agent, or should I say erstwhile agent? For
some unknown reason I have been thinking of you lately. On
Friday, in fact, I was sitting at my desk, and suddenly your
face appeared before me, and truth be told, it was a troubled
face. I thought to myself, 'Where is that young man with all
that power and stage presence? Has he come to his senses
and enrolled in a dental school? Has he married a rich
woman and moved to Connecticut?' As you know, I have an
almost religious belief in these little intuitions of mine, so I
thought I'd call to see if you had overcome the irresponsible
habits such as skipping appointments and insulting pro-
ducers that led to our parting some months ago. If so, I have
a few calls for you to go out on. If interested, ring me up.''

I spent the next few moments in a sort of ironic wonder
at both the tone and the timing of her call. Was this a plot to
torment me? No, I thought, getting up from the couch. It actually made a certain sense. I'd gone over the edge with
Frank, and now I had resurfaced on the other side. I walked
over to the mirror on the closet door and saw a man in his
prime. I had all my strength, most of my passion, and even a
touch of wisdom to go with it. "Edward," I said to the reflec-

tion, "perhaps things are turning around." I laughed, threw two lightning left jabs, an overhand right, and a left hook reminiscent of a young Joe Frazier.

I fell asleep to an image of Charlotte's face, smiling above me. Her eyes were luminous and her skin was perfectly smooth, like a touched-up photograph. And there were cherubs singing in the background.

I called Nate Greenberg first thing Tuesday morning. He said he'd be in my neighborhood that afternoon, around one o'clock, and he'd drop by then. He said it wouldn't take long.

I spent the rest of the morning cleaning up the apartment and doing some light shopping. I called my mother, Laura, and a couple of friends. At twelve-thirty I put up some coffee, smoked a cigarette, and waited for Nate Greenberg. I was a little tense, but feeling okay, like waiting to read at an audition.

He showed up at one-fifteen with another detective, a good-looking black guy of about thirty named Parker. Greenberg was in his late forties. He was medium height, stout, with a thin mustache and dark kinky hair. I sat on the couch, and they sat on two chairs around a card table that I had off the kitchen. We all had coffee, and the atmosphere was almost pleasant. Parker asked the questions:

"How long did you work for Frank Popowski?"

"Did you ever see anyone suspicious around the shop?"

"Did Frank have any enemies that you know of?"

I kept my answers short and simple, my tone somber. I would have felt in complete control except for the way Greenberg kept looking at me. He had one of those faces that always seemed to be smiling. I tend to dismiss people like this out of hand, but not him. He had alert, piercing, dark eyes, and I had the impression that if I asked him what was so funny he'd have a good answer. After about ten questions by Parker there was a quiet moment, and Greenberg spoke.

"You don't seem like a truck driver to me," he said. He looked at the two bookcases against the wall and the smaller one near the bed. "What are you, a writer?"

"I'm an actor," I replied. "On occasion."

He nodded and said, "My niece studies with Uta Hagen."

I nodded back and thought, Big deal.

"I don't think she'll make it, though. She's too fat."

"I'm sorry."

He shrugged. "It wouldn't be such a tragedy. My brother's the biggest electrical contractor in New York. Her allowance could support half the Puerto Ricans in the Bronx."

I raised my eyebrows as if to say, "A full half, huh?"

"I don't agree with bringing up children that way. I think people should work for what they get. A little help from the parents, fine, but Leslie, that's my niece, she lives in a fancy apartment on the East Side, she goes to her father's place in the Hamptons every weekend, I mean where's the incentive? She's a nice girl, though," he concluded sadly.

"Well," I said, "that's important." I had the uneasy sense that there was a method to all this nonsense.

"She'd probably go ape-shit over you," said Greenberg. "Would you like to meet her?"

I was tapping my forefinger against my lip and staring at him. "I don't think so."

He affected an expression of hurt, looked at Parker, who was smiling ironically, and then back to me. "Why not?"

"She's too fat."

His eyes twinkled, and then he exploded with laughter. The sound of him filled the room, but he never took his eyes off me. He came to the end of his outburst and said, "How tight are you and Vincent Minetta?"

"Just a guy I work with," I said easily.

"Have you ever seen him socially, outside of work?"

"Once or twice."

"Where?"

I looked toward the right corner of the ceiling, as if trying to recall. I could feel both their eyes boring into me. "We've been out for drinks, he's been over here. I've been to his house."

"That's once or twice?" asked Greenberg. There was no trace of a smile about him now.

"I didn't mean it literally."

"Obviously," he said drily. "How did you get along with your boss?"

"We got along all right."

"That's not what I heard."

"You've heard wrong," I said. "We may have had arguments here and there, but . . ."

"Arguments about what?" he said, leaning forward in his chair.

I looked at him and cursed myself silently. "Minor things," I said. "Stuff about the truck, the paperwork. A normal conversation with Frank can sound like an argument."

"Not any more," said Parker soberly. "You don't seem to have any remorse. You worked for the guy and he's dead. I don't think you care."

"I care plenty," I told him. "There's all kinds of ways of looking at death."

"And how do you look at it?"

"That's my business."

"Can I get a glass of water?" asked Greenberg politely. I gestured toward the kitchen and watched him shuffle in there. He returned with the water, but instead of sitting back down he moved close to me. "You and that wop, Minetta, offed your boss for a little extra spending money."

"That's not true."

He pointed his finger at me. "I smell a rat here, *boychik,* and you're right in the middle of it. Your friend Vincent's got a sheet that includes two years in Dannemora for armed robbery. He stinks. He did the job on Popowski, and you went along for the ride. I can get you out of this with a slap on the wrist as long as you don't fuck with me."

I shook my head. "You're wrong. I hope you find the guy that did it."

Greenberg took a deep breath and sat back down in his chair. He smiled sadly and shook his head at me. "I know you're lying, but I wish I knew why you were lying. You seem like a smart boy, and this Minetta's not worth it. As a matter of fact, if I was in your position I'd watch my back."

"Thanks for the advice."

"Wise-ass motherfucker," said Parker under his breath.

"Don't mind Parker," said Greenberg kindly. "He's not a happy man. For all his good looks he's got problems with women. The black ones think he's too high falutin', and the white ones don't trust him. Plus he's got one of these really tiny pricks. He takes it all out on his work."

If Parker even heard this he didn't show it. He kept looking at me, a mean, vaguely threatening expression on his face.

They were at the door when Greenberg turned to me. "We'll be seeing you around. Don't leave town."

After shutting the door behind them I walked over to the bed and slumped onto it face down. I imagined a hole in the bed that I could crawl into and be safe and warm. The picture was vivid enough that, for a few minutes, it gave me some comfort.

Vincent lived in a big apartment complex in Coney Island. After the cops left and I'd settled down a bit, I jumped on the D train and went out there.

He wasn't home. I waited in the hallway outside his apartment and smoked a couple of cigarettes. The corridor was outdoors, but fully enclosed by metal grating. From where I was standing I could see the beach and the boardwalk and a good chunk of the ocean. A lot of people passed by in the hallway, and I was struck by how many of them were children and teenagers. It occurred to me that in the Village I rarely saw or noticed kids—was that possible? I could feel a difference in the air; it was in the Brooklyns of the world where real life was lived, people got married, and children were raised. It made me a little sick to think about it, but then I considered Benjamin, and the image of his quick, broad smile worked its usual magic on me. I'm part of this, I thought, as I watched a skinny girl of about twelve walk toward me. She wore a lot of makeup, high heels, and tight jeans: ridiculous, but cute. I smiled at her as she walked by, and, after a tremulous moment, she returned it, exposing two rows of sparkling orthodonture.

I'd been there about a half-hour when I saw Vincent coming up the walkway outside. He was with a skinny Puerto Rican guy with a mustache and a red bandana around his head. They stopped midway down the walk and shook hands, except it wasn't just a handshake; the guy gave him something that Vincent shoved in his pocket. I leaned against the door to his apartment and waited.

He rounded the corner quickly with his head down, and if I hadn't said something he would've walked right into me.

He pulled up and stared at me blankly for a moment, as if he'd just woken from a deep sleep. Then his eyes widened, and he said my name.

"Sorry I didn't call first, but I wanted to talk to you."

"It's cool, it's cool," he said as he opened the door. "You talk to Greenberg?"

I told him the whole story, leaving out only the reference Greenberg made to watching my back around Vincent.

When I was done he shook his head in disgust. "Those motherfuckers. They came down on you because they figured you might crack. You did good, though."

"Yeah, well, I don't even want to think how close I came to cracking. At one point I almost said, fuck this, it's not like I murdered the guy. He was going to kill you."

He gave me a strange, hard look, and then it disappeared. "I gotta take a shit," he said, rubbing his nose. "I'll be right back."

I sat there tapping my fingers on the arm of the chair and reluctantly absorbing Vincent's living room. Cheap, thin carpets of a dull brown, sheets for curtains, and nothing on the walls. There was a slashed-up Naugahyde rocking chair in the far corner and, across from this, presiding arrogantly amid the squalor, was a twenty-five-inch Sony Trinitron.

I was restless, and I was also thirsty. I went into the kitchen and opened the refrigerator. There were two things in there, a half-eaten Hershey's milk chocolate bar and a bottle of ketchup. I found a glass in the cupboard and drank some tap water. On the counter was a metal vial, and on impulse I opened it. Inside was a rolled-up rubber strap, a dropper, a syringe, and a bottle cap. I wasn't shocked exactly, but surprised. I knew Vincent liked to get high, but I didn't know he was this serious about it.

I went back into the living room, and a minute later Vincent returned. He sat across from me on the couch. "Are you pissed off because I never told you about that armed robbery thing?"

I shook my head. "But it did throw me off a little with Greenberg."

He nodded. "Yeah, I spent almost two years up there. All I gotta do is blow my nose at the wrong time and they'll send me back. I would die first. That's why I don't like to hear you say shit like you almost gave yourself up, because you can forget about getting off on some self-defense plea— it's too late for that. When you talk like that it makes me think you'll wake up some morning and decide to clear your conscience. You wouldn't do that, would you?"

I stared at him. His conversational tone only made the malevolence behind it more palpable. "I don't want to go to jail either," I said.

"Good," he said, his voice friendly again. "Then we got no problem."

"And I don't like being threatened."

He shrugged innocently. "I wasn't threatening you, man. I'm just telling you where I'm at. I trust you completely."

"How's everything else?" I asked him.

His eyes dropped. "I don't know," he said. "Julie's gone. It's not easy."

"I see you're doing something for the pain," I said, instantly regretting it.

He looked up at me.

"I saw a set of works in the kitchen."

"I'm holding them for a friend."

"That's nice of you."

He just looked away and nodded sleepily.

"Vincent," I said, "we together on this?"

He made a conciliatory gesture with his arms and said, "All the way, my man. All the way."

5

I lifted my glass toward Charlotte. "Tonight is a night to celebrate."

She raised her own glass and smiled at me. "And what are we celebrating?"

"I got a part on 'Hillsdale.' "

"What's 'Hillsdale'?"

"It's the number-one soap opera on television."

"Are you kidding me?"

I took a deep breath and a quick moment to verify with myself that I hadn't dreamed this. "No, I'm not kidding. It's a temporary thing, though. It's a two-month contract for at least two episodes a week. Seven hundred bucks a shot. After two months they either ditch the character or make it permanent."

She reached out and squeezed my hand. "Eddie, that's fantastic. I'm happy for you, you deserve it."

I looked at her soberly. "You think so?"

She straightened up in her chair and looked at me. "Yes, I think so. Don't you?"

"Yeah, I suppose."

"Is there something wrong?" she asked.

The waiter came over and asked if we needed anything else. We told him no.

I looked down at the table. "It was just strange that it happened now and that it came so easily. I didn't even have to go back for a second call. I read a scene, he asked if I'd be willing to cut my hair, and he gave me the part."

Charlotte was smiling and shaking her head. "Just like that, huh? What's the part like?"

"I play a young psychiatrist who screws his patients and deals drugs on the side."

She laughed. "Sounds terrific."

We grinned at each other across the table.

"Are you happy?" she asked me.

"Almost."

"Only almost?"

"When I'm not with you I have this ache inside. I'm not sure I like it. I'm not sure it's good for me."

She dropped her gaze and then returned it. When she spoke, her voice was emotional. "Maybe we shouldn't see each other for a while."

"Is that what you want?"

"No. But I don't want to make you unhappy, and I don't want to distract you while you're doing this part."

"Noble sentiments," I said.

"You think they're false?" she asked, her eyes hardening.

"Not exactly," I replied. "I just wonder what it is you want for yourself. Everybody wants something for themselves."

"That's very cynical. You're very cynical."

I smiled. "It keeps me going."

"Well," she said, "when you find out what I want then

you let me know. Because I don't seem to be too sure of anything these days."

"Does that include Margaret?"

She looked at me sharply.

"Hey," I said, "can't I use her name?"

"It includes everything," she said.

"Did you tell her about me?"

She nodded sadly.

"How did she take it?"

Charlotte shrugged uneasily. "I don't really know. We
had a marathon talk the other night—about everything. You
were only a part of it. It looks like we're going to be separate
for a while."

"Really?"

"Yeah, I'm going to move out. I didn't want to tell you. I
figured you'd think it was because of you, and it isn't. It's
been building for a long time. I feel like I have to be alone."

I nodded and raised my glass. "A toast."

She raised her own glass, but looked at me suspiciously.
"A toast to what?"

"To Charlotte," I replied. "Alone."

We left the restaurant and began to walk up Sullivan
Street toward the park. I pulled her under an awning and
kissed her. She kissed me back, stiffly at first, and then relaxed and put her arms around my neck.

"I only live three blocks from here," I said.

She put her mouth near my ear. "I can't tonight. I told
you that."

"Oh, yeah," I whispered, pushing her back against the
door. I shoved my hands down the back of her pants and
ground my leg against her crotch while kissing her face and

neck. She started breathing heavily and groaning, but after a few minutes she pushed me away from her and leaned weakly against the door. "I want you inside of me," she said. "Here."

I instinctively glanced over my shoulder. There weren't a lot of people around, but there were some. I looked back at her a bit lamely, and she smiled.

"Not here, stupid." She gestured with her thumb. "In the park."

I shook my head. "Forget it. I don't even walk through that place at night."

She smiled again and came closer to me, putting her hand on the front of my jeans. "What's the matter," she said, squeezing softly. "Scared? A big man like you?"

We sifted our way through the park provoking little attention save the usual offers of joints and cocaine and Quaaludes. We ended up in the children's playground, an enclosed area at the north end. I had spent time here with Benjamin. I could hear the voices of the people in the park as well as those walking on the street almost beside us, yet we were alone.

Charlotte was on the ground and wriggling out of her jeans and panties.

"You have wonderful ideas," I said to her.

"Shut up and take your pants off," she said.

I thought we might do it on the grass under a tree, or maybe even on the bottom part of the slide, but Charlotte insisted on the sandbox.

6

I had shot six episodes of "Hillsdale," three of them had already aired, and I was feeling stronger and more natural in the role each time. The producer was starting to talk about the possible developments for my character, so it looked as if I might be working for a while. The night before, for the first time, Charlotte had stayed over in my apartment. She had brought with her a tattered volume of English literature, and we had read to each other the sonnets of Shakespeare and the poems of Donne and Blake and Wordsworth. Tiring of this, we had turned to each other and made love like gods until dawn. I hadn't heard from the cops in almost two weeks, and the memory of Frank's death was fading like a bad dream.

I had so much energy with no immediate place to put it that I decided to walk the fifty-odd blocks from the studio to home. I walked down Ninth Avenue to Twenty-third Street and across to Broadway and south again. The air was filled with a New-York-only kind of excitement, a hint at unlimited possibilities too large and frightening for any one man, though tonight I felt nearly equal to it.

The fact that I was not equal to it began to emerge when I stopped off at the corner to buy a bottle of Bushmills and the checkout lady, a middle-aged black woman, pointed a finger at me. "You're on 'Hillsdale,' " she said.

"That I am, my dear," I replied, smiling at her and touching her hand. "You like the show?"

"Yes, but I don't like you," she said. "You're not a good man. You're gonna get your comeuppance one day."

I looked into her face expecting to see a smile or a glint in her eyes, but she was serious. I took the bottle out of her hand before she had a chance to put it in the bag. "I'm just an actor," I said to her, and I walked out of the store.

I was still slightly distracted when I got to my building, and the first honk of the horn went right through me, but a second honk turned me around to see Detective Greenberg emerge from a light blue sedan. I felt an immediate tightness in my chest, but I didn't have time to get seriously disturbed because he was upon me. The smile on his face was not quite friendly, but conspiratorial.

"Hiya, Eddie."

"Detective Greenberg," I replied politely.

"Please," he said. "Call me Nate."

Call me Nate. Had he really said that? "I don't think that's necessary."

He laughed and murmured to himself, "He doesn't think that's necessary." He gestured to the car with his thumb. "Get in the car. I wanna talk to you."

As I opened the door to the back seat I took notice of a Latin guy standing across the street with his arms folded. There was something vaguely familiar about the man, but I couldn't place him. I lowered my body into the car, and my nose was bombarded by the smell of stale tobacco and hot vinyl and my ears by the crackling static of the police radio.

Greenberg was sitting sideways in the front seat with his arms folded casually over the backrest. "Why didn't you tell me you were a celebrity?" he asked me.

I shrugged. "It's a temporary role on a soap opera."

His eyebrows shot up as if pulled by a string. "You got a role on a soap opera?"

I hesitated before answering. "I thought that's what you meant."

"Which one is it?" he asked. "I gotta tell my wife."

"It's called 'Hillsdale.' What did you mean when you called me a celebrity?"

He smiled widely, this time more like a proud father, though with a dose of irony. "You're Willie Black's nephew."

I leaned back and closed my eyes. I should have known. I had hardly thought about Willie in years, but I should have known. "You know him?" I asked Greenberg.

"Do I know him?" he said. "I've been a policeman in this town for over thirty years; of course I know him. I knew him before that even, or I knew of him. Where I grew up in the Bronx your uncle was a legend. With the possible exception of Joe DiMaggio, I think Willie Black was the most revered person in the neighborhood." He chuckled at this, and said, "Imagine that, a ballplayer and a mobster."

"I haven't seen him in five years," I said.

He leaned his head forward slightly. "Why not?" he asked.

"No special reason," I replied. "We don't have much in common."

Greenberg shook his head. "You should always stay in touch with family. You never know when you'll need them."

I looked out the window. It was a really beautiful evening, only just now beginning to get dark. Across the street was one of the better-known Off-Broadway theatres, and there were several well-dressed people, mostly couples, near the door. I thought of calling Charlotte, but decided it was too soon after last night; best to let it breathe.

I looked at Greenberg. "Is there anything else?"

"Why, you got plans?" he asked. "You got a hot date?" When I didn't answer, he said, "You're not a faggot, are you?"

I laughed and said, "What if I am?"

He shrugged generously. "No, nothing. I just wouldn't have picked you for one, that's all, but you never know. I read somewhere the other day that this NFL linebacker came out and admitted he was gay."

I leaned forward and put my hand on Greenberg's arm. "Maybe we should continue this upstairs, Nate."

He pulled his arm away instinctively, but when he saw my comic expression he laughed loudly.

"Listen," I said, holding up my hands in mock surrender, "much as I'm enjoying myself I really have to go."

Ignoring this, Greenberg said, "What's he like?"

"What's who like?"

He gestured impatiently. "Willie Black. I mean, what's he like around the house—does he have any hobbies, that kind of stuff."

I looked at Greenberg. "What's going on here?" I asked him. "You work for *People* magazine or something?"

"Shit," replied Greenberg. "*People* magazine would love to do a profile on Willie—they should be so lucky. He's got more balls than all the jerks they've had in there combined. Willie knew all the big boys—Frank Costello, Luciano, Lepke, you name 'em, he did business with them." The detective stopped for a moment and flushed slightly. "I'm a student of organized crime," he said. "Kind of silly I guess, but shit, some guys are interested in baseball stars, I happen to be interested in mobsters. What can I say?"

"You don't have to explain to me," I told him.

"So what's he like?" insisted Greenberg.

His sincerity made me consider the question seriously, but what could I tell him? Willie was, even to me, a shadowy figure. I remembered when I was sixteen and busted for pot, my mother had come apart, and it had been Willie who had to come and bail me out. He'd been tough with me that night, and I had been appropriately contrite, both of us playing a part, and both of us tacitly aware of it. The evening ended in an all-night diner, my indiscretion forgotten, and Willie regaling me with anecdotes about my father and the good old days.

I didn't even know who he was until a couple of years after that. I was browsing in a bookstore, and I picked up a volume on the history of organized crime. In the middle of the book was a picture of Uncle Willie, tanned, healthy-looking, wearing a Hawaiian-style shirt, and smoking a cigar. Underneath the picture it said, "Willie 'Blue Eyes' Black, New York racketeer and crony of Frank Costello."

I had gaped at the photo and then read all of the many references to Willie in the book. I learned he was not a real estate investor as I'd been told, but a former bootlegger, a murderer, an extortionist, and finally an entrepreneur in Las Vegas. I brought the book home to show to my mother, but she wouldn't look at it, which was not hard to understand because since my father's death Willie had footed all the important bills. Better not to think about where the money came from.

Our last meeting had been unpleasant. The occasion had been a request for money for drama school. I couldn't remember the exact amount, but it was no more than a few thousand dollars, and he had turned me down. Planning a career in acting, Willie had said, was stupid, and he didn't throw money away at stupidity. He said he was an investor and it went against his instinct.

It was then, for the one and only time, that we had harsh words. We were in a crowded restaurant in the Village, and I leaned over the table and said, "You think acting is stupid; would it be better if I followed in your footsteps?"

His face clouded over, and I felt a whiff of the viciousness he was known for. "And what do you know about that?"

"I can read."

"You can talk, too," he said. "That doesn't make you smart. You look down your nose at how I make my money, but that doesn't stop you from wanting a piece of it."

All that was left for me was to stalk out of the restaurant. I called him up a few days later to apologize, and he was friendly, pretending nothing had happened.

Greenberg was waiting patiently.

"He's a good guy, I think. Down to earth—generous."

Greenberg nodded happily. "Most of those guys are. It's amazing. Show me a guy with the lily-white super-clean record and half the time there's your sicko, there's your child molester, your wife-beater, et cetera. And then you turn around and take a guy like Willie who's probably had a hundred guys blown away, and he's a good family man, a guy you can have a drink with, a guy you can trust. What does that tell you?" He waited for my answer.

"I don't know," I said. "You've probably had more experience with that kind of stuff than I have."

He nodded. "Yeah, but I haven't read as many books as you have. I remember those bookcases upstairs. Have you really read all those books?"

"Some of them."

He shook his head in wonder. "I was looking at your books that day. I couldn't even pronounce half the fuckin' titles. You must be smart."

I kept my mouth shut and watched him.

"If you're so smart then why the hell are you protecting

Vincent Minetta? He's a loser. We know he did it. It's just a matter of time. I can get you immunity if you tell me now."

I shook my head slowly. I was surprised how calm I felt. "I have no idea what happened to Frank."

He held my gaze for a moment and then smiled, retreating. "Okay, Willie Black's nephew. That's all for now, but I'll be back."

"You'll be back?"

"Sure."

"Can you call first next time?"

He laughed and pointed a finger at me. "I like you. I really do."

I was at the door when he called my name. I turned, and he was standing near the car with something in his hand. It was the bottle of Bushmills I'd just bought. "Here," he yelled, and he threw the bottle underhand about seven feet in the air toward me. I watched the bottle come at me end over end and I held my hands out to catch it, but I had it badly misjudged and the bottle grazed through my fingers and shattered on the ground. I jumped back into the door to avoid the glass and the liquor.

Greenberg smiled sympathetically and said, "No hands, you got no hands."

I turned away from him and pulled the keys out of my pocket. No hands my ass. I had great hands—quick, too. What the fuck did Greenberg know about it? The fat bastard.

When I got upstairs I took a shower. In my bathrobe, I sat on the bed and stared out the one window of my apartment. In the twilight, or at any other time, the view was uninspiring: a windowless, brick side wall of the adjacent building.

What to think of Greenberg? One moment an ominous force to be reckoned with and the next moment a buffoon. If I got him Willie's autograph would he leave me alone?

There was something else bothering me, something I couldn't identify until suddenly a connection was made between my brain and the ugly wall outside. Was the man I'd seen across the street a few minutes ago the same one I had seen in Brooklyn with Vincent? Neither time had I gotten a close-up view, but there was a definite physical resemblance, and not only in size and coloring, but in the body, the legs, the way the man stood, even the tilt of the head. I shivered inwardly and wondered:

Would Vincent consider killing me rather than returning to jail?

People consider all kinds of things.

Would he do it?

I reclined in bed and let the possibilities consume me. Terrible things, but I was able to maintain a strange sort of equilibrium about it. After a while, I slept, but it wasn't a sleep like any I'd ever had before. It was wary, weightless, like an animal in a jungle.

7

"Just what is it you want from me?" I asked.

"I want you to leave my sister alone," said Emily.

I went to pour myself a drink and looked into the second camera. "She's a big girl," I said.

"I don't trust you," she said to me. "Suzanne is weak, she's lonely; perfect prey for someone like you."

"What do you mean someone like me?" I asked her. "You sound as if I'm some sort of vermin."

"That's about right," she snapped. "You're an immoral opportunist. You're after Daddy's money, you think I can't see that?"

I moved my arms in a gesture of wounded pride. "Emily, I'm a professional man, a psychiatrist. My income is adequate."

She shook her head and smiled viciously. "Oh, no, I know about you. I know about your gambling debts and your alimony payments. You have expensive tastes, Dr. Stone, and quite a past; I'm finding out more every day."

I took a step back and surveyed her speculatively. My nose itched, and I scratched it.

"Cut!" yelled the voice from the back. "What the fuck was that?"

"Real life," I retorted. "Remember that?"

"Eight thousand bucks an hour, motherfucker. That's real life. Pick your nose on your own time."

I surveyed Emily speculatively. "I see you're doing your homework."

"Oh, yes," she said. "And what an interesting assignment it is."

"This is all very clear to me."

"What do you mean?"

"Oh, well," I replied knowingly, "it must be difficult for you to watch your sister get involved in a healthy relationship. It's common knowledge in Hillsdale why Harry left you for that barmaid."

"You bastard!" she seethed. "I don't need your dimestore analysis. What do you know about it?"

"What do I know about it?" I asked, walking over to her. I looked over her shoulder at the tape machine and read the next line. "I know about needs, Emily, needs that we all have." I stroked the side of her face lightly. "You ought to find someone to satisfy your needs—maybe then you could relax—maybe then you could smile once in a while."

I continued stroking her, but when I moved in for the kiss she tried to slap me across the face. I caught her hand and pushed her roughly down on the couch. I leaned over, my face close to hers, and said, "There are certain things I want, Emily, and I'm going to get them. Suzanne happens to be one of those things, and if you get in my way you'll be sorry. I'm not one of your fancy, soft, Hillsdale boys. I don't play the same games. I don't play games at all."

"Cut!" yelled the voice from the back. "Not bad. A born prick if I ever saw one. That's it for today. Eight o'clock tomorrow morning I want everyone here."

I started to walk off the set when he yelled to me again. "Hey, Eddie, you gonna pick your nose now?"

"Yeah," I replied. "Your mama wants an early dinner."

As I put the key in the lock I could hear my phone ringing. Probably Charlotte, I thought. We had talked of getting together tonight.

I picked up the phone and said, "Hi."

"Hi," she replied.

"Oh, man," I said. "I get a hard-on just hearing your voice. Did you move into your new place yet?"

"Eddie?" replied the voice, now faltering. "This is Julie, Julie Minetta."

"Oh," I said, after a moment. "I'm sorry, Julie. I thought it was somebody else."

She giggled and said, "Yeah."

"How are you?" I asked. I tried to picture her. Was she even twenty years old? The couple of times I'd seen her she'd had on too much makeup and dressed like a greaser, but Julie was a genuine beauty: large, striking brown eyes, thick black hair almost to her waist, and a body that was almost unfashionably full. I hadn't talked to her much because in Vincent's presence she'd always been the polite young wife, but even at that I had sensed an unhappy restlessness, even a kind of ambitiousness about her.

"I'm okay," she said. "Pretty good, actually. But I kind of wanted to talk to you. I'm worried about Vincent."

Me too, I thought. "Go ahead, talk."

She hesitated. "Not on the phone. I go to school in the city now. I thought maybe if you had some time, maybe just an hour or so . . ."

An alarm went off somewhere in the back of my head.

Don't do it, I thought. Make her talk on the phone. "Does Vincent know you're calling me?"

"No," she replied. "He's very proud, Eddie. I don't think he'd like it."

"Yeah, well, I'm supposed to be seeing him myself this weekend. Also, I'm kind of busy with this soap now . . ."

"I know," she blurted merrily. "I think you're a great actor."

"You do?"

"Yeah, I really really do. When you walk on the screen it's really powerful."

I felt a mild chill of appreciation, but I responded casually. "That's just because you know me, Julie."

"No," she said. "I watched the last show with a couple of girlfriends. We all agreed—it was like watching Brando or somebody."

Brando. I lingered for a moment over the name, the face, the style. The comparison was a little far-fetched, but I could see it.

"Well," I said tentatively. "I don't work on Tuesday. I suppose sometime on Tuesday . . ."

"Tuesday's great for me," said Julie. "My last class is over at five."

"Five?" I felt queasy, weak. "We could have dinner."

"All right," she said. "That would be nice."

"Call me after your class," I said. "We'll meet somewhere."

I hung up the phone and sat on the bed, staring out the window. The wall outside was still ugly, still indifferent, but now I projected images on its face. Vincent, Julie, Greenberg, even Charlotte, all in their turn I pondered them. It was really just a game I was playing with myself, but then there was a fuzziness, almost like a television station on the blink, followed by a new face, Frank Popowski. His expression was one I had never seen on him in life. It was soft, reverent, and more than just sympathetic, more like pitying. The image was vivid enough to chill me and set my heart pounding. I closed my eyes and breathed evenly for a moment, and when I opened them he was gone.

I had a shot of whiskey and a beer, and then I called Charlotte.

"Well," she said, "if it isn't the notorious, the rakish, the devastating Dr. Stone."

I responded with a grunt. "I take it you saw one of the shows."

"Yes," she replied drily. "You deserve a medal for being able to read those lines with a straight face."

"Some people," I said, in mock stuffiness, "have a considerably higher opinion of my work." I thought of Julie's enthusiasm. A younger mind, uncluttered by needless complexities.

"Yeah," said Charlotte, "and some people are stupid."

"Who knows," I replied. "Maybe 'Hillsdale' is the real art of our time, and all that serious stuff is irrelevant."

I heard her exhale, and then she said, "God, that's a depressing thought."

"Charlotte, I really like your writing."

"Eddie," she replied, mimicking my tone perfectly, "don't patronize me."

After a silence, she said, "I got something published."

"Not to patronize," I said, "but that's great."

"Yeah, it's nice. It's small press and no money, but it's a good magazine, and I think a few people will read it."

"I'll read it."

"You already have. It's the one you read in the car."

"Oh, yeah, that was good. Tell me something—was that based on you and Margaret?"

"Oh, God," she replied impatiently. "What a dumb question."

"Why is it dumb?"

"It just is. What are you doing tonight?"

"I'm free. How about you?"

"I have some things to do, but I wanted to invite you over later, around twelve. I thought you'd help me christen my new apartment."

"A christening," I murmured, savoring the image. "I love religious rituals."

8

We had trouble agreeing on a place to meet. Vincent didn't want to come to Manhattan, and I didn't want to go to Brooklyn, so we ended up at a neighborhood bar in Queens off Metropolitan Avenue—a two-fare trip for both of us. Five years ago I'd been part of the construction crew that got the place ready to open. I became friends with the owner, and I used to drink here once in a while. Ownership had changed hands several times since; at first it was called Rat's, then Tommy's, then Cat's, and now Ethel's. My friend Johnny had gone on to bigger and better things. He owned a string of massage parlors in the city now, drove a Rolls-Royce, and still drank a quart of vodka a day.

Rat's was the perfect name for the place. It was small, ugly, and, above all, anonymous. It was Sunday afternoon, and the only other patrons were two old guys in front, at the bar itself. They were blue-collar types, but retired, heavy boozers. The lifeblood of your neighborhood bar, as Johnny used to say. Behind the bar was a fat blond woman of indeterminate age. She sat on a stool watching bowling on a black-

and-white television set. Vincent and I were sipping beers at a table in the rear.

"I'm really happy for you, man," he said, shaking his head. "I mean the guy I worked with in the same truck for six months is on TV—a fuckin' celebrity. Maybe I should've put a blade to Frank—then maybe my life would have gone up, too."

"It's not funny," I said sharply.

"Funny?" he said sarcastically. "Who said anything about funny? It sure as hell ain't funny to me. It was you lost your head, you offed the fuckin' guy."

"He was going to kill you," I whispered. "I was protecting you."

Vincent waved his hand, dismissing the idea. "He wasn't killing anybody. You had to know Frank."

"I don't want to talk about it."

"Of course you don't want to talk about it. You're on TV fucking housewives. I'm out of work, out of my marriage, out of life."

"Shit," I said. "You sound like a soap opera yourself. Don't blame me for your problems."

He turned away and took some of his beer. He looked terrible. His face was white and pasty, eyes dull, and every thirty seconds or so he'd scratch his nose or some other part of his face.

"You ever think about that, Eddie? I mean, ever since it happened things went up for you. Before, we were sort of at the same place, just working together. Now . . ." His voice trailed off.

I took a deep breath and said, "You gotta stop this, Vincent. You're losing it. I don't know if it's Julie or that garbage you put up your veins, but you gotta get your head on straight."

"My head's on straighter than ever," he retorted. "What makes people nervous is that for once I'm looking out for my own ass first. I'm through with bad luck, man. I'm ready for some good luck even if I have to make it for myself."

"Bullshit," I said. "You look like a junkie, you talk like a junkie, you even smell like a junkie. Your wife left you, and you're getting high to ease the pain, admit it."

He looked at me and shook his head as if dealing with a child. "First of all," he said, "I been fucking with dope for twelve years and never got into anything I couldn't get out of, so save your sermon. And as far as Julie's concerned, it's just a part of my life that's over. She needed to get away from her stepfather, and there I was. I had a job, my own place, the whole bit. That's all it ever was, man, I see that now."

I shook my head sadly. "I remember you telling me the story of when you met and you ran away to Florida and you talked and screwed for three days straight without sleeping. I mean, I was sitting in the truck and wondering if I was ever really in love. People can't fake that kind of thing, Vincent. That was part of it, too."

He looked at me thoughtfully and was about to speak when the bartender came over and asked if we wanted another beer. We told her not yet, and she smiled at me oddly and then returned to the bar.

"I don't know, man," said Vincent. "I think that people look out for themselves first, and then they do what they do after that. One thing about prison, and I know it's an old line, but you really have time to think. I used to lie on my bed and think all day long sometimes, and mostly I thought about people and all the sugar they talk and all the shit they do. I used to get so depressed I wanted to kill myself, and it wasn't because I was in jail either, it didn't even have much to do

with my own situation, but how fucked up things really are.
That's what scares me about going back—all that time and
all that thinking."

"Don't worry about it," I said. "Because you're not
going back."

"I hope not," he replied. "This Greenberg motherfucker
worries me, though. I don't like the way he keeps coming
back to you. Maybe he has some evidence, I don't know."

"He thinks you did it."

Vincent shook his head. "That's what he says he thinks.
What he really thinks is something else. The important thing
is he doesn't get a confession."

"Who's going to confess?"

"Not me," he said.

"Not me either."

He nodded and sipped his beer.

"You don't believe me, do you?"

"I don't know what I believe, man. The only thing
seems sure to me is that I got a history of bad luck and a history of being screwed over by guys with good luck, guys like
you."

I leaned back in my chair and took a deep breath. "Is
that why you're having me followed?"

He looked at me curiously.

"I sensed I was being followed last week. I had the idea
it might be you."

He leaned over and said, "You *sensed* you were being
followed? You had the idea it was me? What kind of bullshit
is that?"

"I don't know," I replied, rubbing my forehead. I decided not to be any more specific. "It's just a feeling I had."

Vincent raised his eyebrows and whistled softly. "Look
who's going crazy now. I thought I was bad."

Okay, I thought. Maybe he's right—an overactive imagination. But maybe he was wrong, maybe he was lying.

"We have no choice," I said. "We have to trust each other."

Vincent gazed toward the front of the bar and whispered, "I'm so fucking scared, man. I wish this hadn't happened."

A single stream of sunlight came through the glass of the front door and illuminated the bald heads of the two men hunched over the bar. They looked like twin turtles. In my imagination I saw them when they were younger, with full heads of hair, bright eyes, and erect bodies. "Me too," I said to Vincent. "Me too."

9

Dinner with Julie was pleasant enough. We ate at a place called Amelia's, less than a block from my apartment. It was a bar-restaurant frequented by Off-Broadway theater people. I could have chosen something quieter, but Amelia's offered its own kind of privacy—everyone there talked, no one ever seemed to listen.

Julie was much different from what I remembered. She'd cut her hair short, in a modern sort of look, with a wave on top. She didn't wear any makeup and dressed carelessly in jeans, sneakers, and a bulky sweater. As she chattered on about school and her plans to move to the city, I couldn't help but think that she knew what she was doing in leaving Vincent. She had turned from caterpillar to butterfly.

As for Vincent, she didn't tell me anything I didn't know, except that he was driving his uncle's taxicab three nights a week. She said that he was despondent, taking drugs, and given to fits of temper. She felt that he respected me and would listen if I talked to him. I told her that I doubted that, but I'd do what I could.

Mostly we talked of other things. She was considering

acting as a career, and she wanted to know all about it from me. I took a negative tack, telling her how tough and disappointing it could be, but it only made her more interested and impressed.

"Are all these people actors?" she asked, looking around.

"A lot of them are."

"They all look so happy."

She was right about that, I supposed. It was the typically noisy scene here—all the men seemed to speak in dramatic baritones and the women in loud, nearly hysterical voices. What is it with me, I wondered, that I find all this passion so distasteful?

I didn't find Julie distasteful. She was probably the youngest and certainly the most striking woman at Amelia's. She went to the ladies' room at one point, and I noticed with amusement that several of the men actually stopped talking long enough to ogle her. She had the sort of body that's lovely to look at, but you wouldn't want your daughter to have one.

Her manner toward me was a shade more than friendly. A few times as she spoke she put her hand on my leg, and once or twice she tried to hold me to a significant gaze, but I didn't respond.

"I'm really attracted to you," she said artlessly, over coffee.

I smiled and averted my eyes.

"I'm sorry," she said. "I have no tact sometimes. I have to learn tact."

"Don't worry about it," I replied, smiling. "I'm just not very open right now—I have a lot on my mind."

She nodded, her large brown eyes searching mine, and giving me the faintly uncomfortable sense that she understood what I was talking about.

"You know," she said, fingering her coffee cup, "sometimes I feel that my three years with Vincent was another lifetime. I mean it's *so* over."

"Yeah," I said, signaling for the check. "I know what you mean."

It was a beautifully still night with just a touch of crispness in the air, a crispness that signaled the end of summer. There were three theatres on the block, but since it was just after eight, the street was virtually deserted.

"I have to call my roommate," said Julie. "Can I use your telephone?"

I almost said yes out of an automatic politeness, but stopped myself. "Julie," I said, smiling awkwardly, "there's a telephone in the restaurant."

"Oh," she said quickly, turning to go back in. But then she walked back to me. "You're not being very nice, you know."

I was at a loss for words, but managed to mumble something to the effect that I was sorry. She went into the restaurant, but returned a moment later.

"Listen, there's like five people waiting. I don't want to hold you up." She held out her hand in a businesslike way and said, "Thanks for dinner."

We said goodbye, but I didn't move. I felt bad about the way I'd treated her, or maybe I just wanted to look at her again; whatever the reason, I stepped up to the door and peered through the glass.

Julie was waiting on a line. There were four people in front of her. I started to feel worse about the whole thing because the plan was for me to walk her to her subway which was up by Union Square Park, a rough area.

I went inside and over to her. "I want you to use my phone," I said.

"It's okay," she replied. "I can wait. It's no problem."
"Come on," I said. "Use my phone, and then I'll walk
you to the train."

While Julie made her call I sat on the couch and flipped
on the television. I recognized the movie right away—*Experiment in Terror* with Glenn Ford and Lee Remick. There
was a dark-haired woman smoking a cigarette and talking to
Glenn Ford on the telephone. Glenn Ford told her not to
worry, he'd be there in an hour.

Julie hung up the phone and said, "It's busy. I gotta
wait a minute or two."

"Want a drink?" I asked her.

"Nah," she said. "Want to smoke a joint?"

"Sure."

She sat on the other end of the couch, and we smoked
and watched. The dark-haired woman was in her bedroom,
getting undressed. She was in her bra and slip and she made
a motion below the camera and then her slip and panties
were in her hand. A nice touch, I thought. I didn't smoke pot
often anymore, and when I did the effect was pretty strong. I
could feel the familiar weight over my eyelids and the pleasant, slowed-down effect on my consciousness. I looked over
at Julie. She was on her haunches with her legs curled up
under her.

"What's the movie?" she asked.

I told her, and she said, "I love old movies."

The woman on the screen was in her bathrobe, and she
was walking around her mannequin-filled apartment because she thought she'd heard a noise.

Julie said, "You must notice things when you watch a
movie that other people don't."

"Not really."

Julie went back to the telephone. She sat there after dialing for what seemed like a long time, and then she put the receiver down hard and said, "Shit."

"Why do you have to call your roommate?" I asked.

She came back to the couch. "She has my keys."

The woman in the movie had returned to the bedroom, and the camera focused on a cluster of mannequins in the living room. One of the "mannequins" moved and then slowly made his way toward the bedroom. Commercial.

"What are you going to do?" I asked Julie.

"I don't know. I don't want to inconvenience you. I know you're not comfortable having me here."

"That's not true," I said quickly. There was an absurd kind of sincerity in my voice. "Wait a little while, then call her again."

She looked at me oddly, and then smiled. "You wanna do some coke?"

I meant to decline, because I never even liked cocaine that much, but something stopped me, and then I decided it would provide a nice balance to the grass, which was already beginning to make me weary.

Julie proceeded to set it all up on a little mirror, and we each did two lines. I sat back and enjoyed the tingle.

Glenn Ford had finally arrived with his partner at the apartment. I remembered how the scene ended, with the woman dead, hanging upside down from the ceiling with the mannequins. I didn't want to see it so I flipped the TV off.

"What's wrong?" asked Julie.

"I'm not in the mood for violence."

"What are you in the mood for?"

"I don't know," I said, turning my body toward her and

putting my knees on the couch. The dark skin of her face looked so smooth and rich and fine that I reached over and stroked her cheek lightly with my finger.

Julie watched me calmly, and when I had removed my hand she asked me if I wanted to sleep with her. There was something about the way she said it, something matter-of-fact and "adult" about it, that broke the spell for me and got me thinking again.

I leaned back and said, "Too many complications."

"Like what?"

"Like the obvious," I replied.

There was an uncomfortable silence, during which I hoped she would leave. I was going to suggest that she call her roommate again, but that would have been rude.

"You and Vincent are in some kind of trouble together, aren't you?"

There it is, I thought. "What makes you say that?"

"Because I'm not blind," she snapped. "And I'm not stupid like you think!"

"Who said anything about stupid?"

"You didn't have to say anything, I can tell. You think I'm cheap dumb trash, but I'm not. You think you're too good for anybody because you're on some stupid TV show, and you know what else?"

"What?"

She paused to allow the statement its full effect: "You're nowhere near as good an actor as Marlon Brando."

I looked at her incredulously for a second, and then I stood up in front of her. "Hold it," I said, "just hold it."

She stared at her lap in a pout.

"Now what did Vincent tell you about us being in trouble?"

"Why should I tell you?"

"Because I'm asking," I replied, and the menacing tone in my voice was as natural as rain.

Julie stared up at me with fearful eyes. She looked like a child who had just done something wrong and didn't yet know the consequences, except that they would be bad.

I spoke again, this time slowly and deliberately. "Tell me what you know, Julie."

She hemmed and hawed for a second and then started to talk in a small, scared voice. "Vincent didn't really tell me anything, but it was the way he acted when he came home that night. I mean he was crazy and it freaked me out. He hugged me real hard, but then he wouldn't talk to me. He sat on the floor in a corner, and he was shaking and crying and saying he was going back to jail. He used your name a couple of times, too, but I couldn't understand what he was talking about. When I asked him what was going on he yelled at me like some crazy. I thought he was going to kill me. I was so scared I went to my mother's house for like three hours, and when I got back he was gone. I didn't see him for two days, but I read about Frank Popowski in the newspaper because Frank lived in our neighborhood."

Mesmerized, I watched her face as she spoke, listening intently to each word. When she was done, I said, "That's it? That's all he said, that he was going back to jail?"

"Yes, that's all he said," snapped Julie. "I know he killed Frank. You don't have to protect him—not from me."

The lie was so intolerable to my ears that my own words came automatically. "He didn't kill Frank," I said. "I did."

As if in slow motion, her head rose and her eyes focused on me. There was no recrimination in her expression, no fear or sympathy, no emotion at all, just a sincere sort of curiosity.

"We got into a fight with Frank over money," I began. I started to tell Julie the story, and as I talked I became less and less aware of her, and more and more aware of the images of the killing that were filling my head. My words became gradually less intelligible, but the reality of the act loomed larger and more clear. It was like watching myself in a movie, but a thousand times more intense. When I was done, my mouth was parched, I was sweating, and my stomach was in knots. But I also felt as if some weight had been lifted off me.

I got up and went into the bathroom. My face, my whole body, was hot, as if I had a fever, and I stood in front of the sink and splashed cold water on my face and chest. I sat down heavily on top of the toilet seat and tried to collect myself. There was something vaguely comforting about being in the bathroom, a world apart, with nothing but basic, functional hygiene equipment. I didn't want to leave, and the thought of ending things right here (perhaps with a razor) fluttered pleasantly through my mind.

There was a knock on the door, and Julie's voice came to me like a sound from another world.

"Eddie, are you okay?"

"Yeah, I'll be right out."

She was standing in the middle of the room.

"Julie, I'm sorry we got into this."

"Don't worry about me, Eddie," she said seriously. "I feel sorry for both you guys. Maybe it did you good to tell someone."

I swallowed hard as I stared at the swell of her breasts and hips. She turned away from me and went to the telephone.

"No," I said, without deciding to.

She turned around and looked at me.

"Don't go," I said. "Don't leave me alone."

I went over and put my arms around her. She leaned

her head against my shoulder, and I gradually let myself as-similate the different parts of her body against mine.

"It feels good," she whispered in my ear. "It feels good."

I undressed her slowly, hoping all the while that she would resist and send me away. When she was naked I laid her flat on the bed, and with a meticulous fascination I ran my hand up and down the length of her, lingering here and there until she said my name and started to grab my clothes. I undressed quickly and slipped into her in one perfect move-ment. She gasped, and in the pain of pleasure I said, "Oh, God," finishing the phrase to myself, "help me."

10

It was just after nine the next morning when I opened my eyes. It hadn't been a dream because Julie was right there on the other side of the bed, still asleep. I lay there, in an exhausted state of physical health, and gazed at her smooth back and the flamboyant flare of her hips. If our coming together was problematic, it wasn't for any lack of physical consonance, though when I thought about it some more I couldn't really be sure how it had been for her. I had fucked, not with the tenderness of a lover, but with the force and tirelessness of a madman.

Before the practical, the ambiguous, and the consequential could settle in on me, I left the bed and took a long and thoughtless shower.

When I returned to the room in my bathrobe, Julie was up. She was sitting at the desk in a bulky sweater, combing her hair. She looked at me tentatively, almost as if expecting to be scolded. I smiled and said, "Good morning."

She brightened a little and said, "Hi."

While I got dressed Julie took her own shower. She came out of the bathroom fully clothed and looking a little sad.

"How you feeling?" I asked her.

She nodded quickly, and I sensed that she didn't trust her voice.

I went over to her and touched her lightly on the shoulder. "Are you okay?"

She looked at me for a second and burst into tears. I took her into my arms and stroked the back of her head as she cried on my shoulder. When she'd calmed down a little I set her in front of me and wiped at her tears. We stared at each other intently, and the next second we were both laughing.

"How about breakfast," I said.

"Great."

There was a Greek coffee shop down the street. Julie and I sat in a booth and ordered pancakes. We made only small talk as we ate until Julie said, "Are you glad I stayed over?"

I took a sip of coffee and said, "Yeah, I think so. Maybe I shouldn't be, but I am."

"You're involved in a lot of guilt, aren't you?"

I looked at her curiously, wondering what book she got that one from. "Julie," I said, with a trace of patronage, "if I'm involved in a lot of guilt, it's for a good reason."

After a silence, I said, "How about you, are you glad?"

She seemed to look past me as she spoke. "It was really good. Seemed like you stayed hard all night. Is it always like that for you?"

"No," I replied, smiling with some embarrassment, "it must have been something in the air."

She looked at me for a long moment, and there was quiet confidence about her now. "What do you think will happen?" she asked.

"You mean," I said, taking a deep breath, "with us?"

"No, not with us," she said softly. "With Frank, and Vincent."

"Oh," I said, looking away from her and out the window. "I think it's going to blow over. Vincent will get himself together, I'll get myself together, and we'll live not quite happily ever after."

"Maybe in the future," said Julie, staring at the table with a mischievous smile on her face, "we can see each other again."

"Julie," I said, feeling a feverishness around my face and eyes, "turn around slowly and tell me if you recognize the guy with the yellow shirt by the newsstand."

She did as I told her, and when she turned back to me her face was beet red. "It's Luis," she said.

"Who is Luis?"

"He's Vincent's dope connection. Did he see us?"

"He saw us," I replied. "He's been following me." I got up from the table. "I'll be right back. You wait here."

Luis was walking down the street with a newspaper folded under his arm; a skinny guy wearing black pants and shoes and the yellow cotton shirt. I caught up to him at the big liquor store on the corner.

"Luis."

He froze for a split second at the sound of his name, but then kept on walking until I got in front of him and blocked his path. He had a thin mustache and some pimples around his nose. He was mean-looking in a slimy kind of way.

"What's going on?" I said.

"Keep walking, gringo," he said. "I don't know you."

"Yes you do," I replied quickly. I could feel a wild anger rise up in me. "Tell Vincent to go fuck himself."

"Vincent?" he said, smiling. "I don't know no Vincent—and I don't know his wife."

I stepped closer to him and pointed my finger. "Stay away from me, you greasy bastard."

His smile ended slowly and was replaced by an expression of flat hatred. "You don't want me, gringo. You don't want any part of me." He parted his shirt near the waist so I could see the leather handle of the knife he had stuck through his belt. "I'll slice your ass up five ways to Sunday."

I took a step back, and our eyes locked in a violent loathing. There was an intrusive voice, and both Luis and I instinctively looked toward it. A few guys working on the roof of the liquor store were watching us, quiet excitement on their faces. One of them, a barrel-chested man of about fifty, stepped forward. "Hey, what's going on down there?"

Luis was already moving. He turned his head to me as he walked and said, "I'll catch you later, my man."

I walked back to the restaurant, my legs, my whole body inwardly fluttering. Julie was still at the booth, an expression of intense concern on her face. "What's happening, Eddie?"

I wasn't able to speak. I grabbed the check off the table and went to the cashier. When we were outside, Julie grabbed my arm.

"What's going on?" she demanded.

"I can't talk about it," I said weakly, not looking at her.

She pulled my arm tighter. "Be careful," she said urgently. "Luis is mean. There's stories about him. He killed someone once."

I turned to face her, removing her hand from my arm. "So did I." For a split second I was appalled at my own words, but then it seemed to fall into place. "So did I."

I went quickly back to the apartment, lighted a cigarette, and paced the room. When I'd calmed down a little I went to the telephone and called my mother. I was to bring Benjamin to see her later in the week, and after confirming that, I said casually, "Does Uncle Willie still live in Queens?"

"Yes, of course," she replied. "Why?"

"Just curious. What's his number?"

"What do you want with his number?"

"Listen," I said, "you're always saying how I never get in touch with family, and now you're hassling me because I want the telephone number of my uncle."

"Are you in some kind of trouble?"

"No. Gimme the number."

I had a pen, but no paper nearby, so I wrote it down on the palm of my hand.

"Eddie, is there anything you need?" she asked.

The genuineness of her concern brought on a rush of emotion inside me, and I spoke to her in a hoarse whisper. "No thanks, Ma, I'm fine."

I stared at the number on my hand for a few minutes, but I didn't dial it. If I went to Willie I'd have to tell him everything, and whatever he was, he was family. No one had tried to hurt me, and even Luis's threat was one that I had provoked. Just be cool, I told myself, just be cool.

There was a white envelope lying on top of the desk. Julie had left the cocaine—a nice gesture, I thought. There was a good deal in there, more than both of us had used last night. I went into the kitchen for a straw and then killed the coke in three mammoth snorts. I sat very still as my head expanded and everything else sort of drifted away. Things are going to work out, I told myself. Then I transferred Willie's number from my hand to a slip of paper and stuck the paper in my wallet.

Part Three

11

"What are you doing here?" I asked sharply. "Can't you see I'm busy?"

Emily stood in front of the desk, undaunted. "I want to know how your first wife died," she said evenly. "I understand the circumstances were, shall we say, questionable. There's a Detective Burton in New York City who still thinks you threw her off that balcony. They just couldn't prove it."

I shook my head and smiled suavely. The lights on the set were even hotter than usual, and I had the impulse to rip the suffocating three-piece suit from my body.

"You've been a busy little girl, haven't you, Emily?"

"Oh, yes," she replied in a quiet hatred. "Elizabeth was a perfume heiress, and you got plenty out of that one. So now you've decided to move to oil, but when my father finds out about all this he'll run you out of town on a rail. No matter what Suzanne says."

"You're wrong, Emily," I said flatly. "You're wrong about me, and you're wrong about Suzanne. We love each other. That's something you can't understand, but it's true, and there's nothing in the world you or anyone else can do about it."

"Oh, yes there is!" she shouted. Her hand went into her purse and emerged with a long, shiny hunting knife.

I felt a wave of nausea as I looked at her and tried to remember my line.

"Cut!" yelled the voice from the back. "Come on, Eddie, you're slow. You're supposed to stand up when she pulls the knife. And spare us the deep breaths, please. You're supposed to be a cold-blooded guy."

When I stood up, the room started to spin. I stared at the knife. "What are you doing with that?"

"I will not stand by," seethed Emily, "and watch my sister fall prey to some cheap adventurer. I've ruined my own life, but I won't let Suzanne ruin hers."

I moved partially around the desk and toward Emily. "Put that away."

"Cut!" came the voice again. "You're out of position, Eddie. Please move back behind the line."

I repeated my line, and Emily took a step forward. "I hate you," she said.

I looked down at the letter opener on the desk and paused as the camera moved in for a close-up. When I picked it up I seemed to lose contact with everything except the feel of the cool metal in my hand. My next line was, "Emily, I'm warning you."

I got to the word "Emily" but no further. The next thing I was conscious of was the thin rug beneath my back, a pain in the side of my head, and the distant, out-of-focus face of Doris, the actress who played Emily.

"How long was I out?" I barely had the strength to ask the question, but I had to know.

"About five seconds."

I became aware of several people, many people, probably
the entire cast and crew, just behind Doris and staring at me.
They all gradually came into focus, but my perception of
them was paranoid.

"Get out of here!" I yelled. "Get the fuck out of here."

I went on like that for a few more seconds, and then it
seemed as if everyone had disappeared except for Larry, the
director. He had his hand firmly on my shoulder and was
looking into my eyes calmly.

"Hey hey hey," he said softly. "You okay?"

I lifted my head slightly and looked around. The set
lights had been turned off, and the only people around were
stage crew and they were going about their own business. I
took a deep breath and looked at Larry. "Yeah," I said. "I'm
okay."

He helped me up, and I stood in the middle of the stage
for a moment. I put my hand to the side of my head, where
there was a good-sized lump but no blood.

"Come on," said Larry, "I want to talk to you."

I followed him off the set and down a hallway to his office. By the time we got there I had my jacket and vest off and
my shirt halfway unbuttoned. He had a sink, and I threw
some cold water on my face and chest. I still felt weak and
rubbery, but my head was clear and no more nausea. I
grabbed a Camel off his desk and settled into an ugly green
leather chair.

Larry claimed to be forty-seven, but he was probably
closer to sixty. He had grayish hair, a toupee up front, and
one of those little goatees that you don't see too often anymore. He was a Polish Jew by way of the Bronx—a hard-
nosed professional on the one hand and something of a flake
on the other. He was a shameless name-dropper, and he liked
to tell stories about his early life in Poland: how his father was

a prince before the Nazis came, and how he, Larry, fought in the Warsaw ghetto. The stories were too numerous, dramatic, and self-serving to be true, but Larry was endearing and entertaining enough that it didn't seem to matter.

He stood over his desk and made a pretense of looking at some papers. Then he shot me a hard glance and said, "You look like shit. You've looked like shit for more than a week."

I sat politely silent and waited.

"I don't like to get involved in the personal problems of the cast," he continued. "Unless those personal problems become professional ones.

"I know your agent, Dolores, for a long time, so I know your history. Some people are afraid of success. Every time they get near it they fuck up. And you're near it." He made a gesture upward with his thumb. "They like you, Eddie, and the people like you, too. You're getting more mail than anyone on the show except for Suzanne.

"You've got plenty to learn, but you've got something." He moved his hand looking for the right word. "A presence on camera like you don't give a shit, only it comes across strong. The only thing worries me," he laughed shortly, "is I don't think you're acting."

Despite the serious and weighty tone of his words I was having a hard time getting into it. Both Larry and the whole office seemed very small and distant, and I felt as if he was talking about someone else.

"Is it drugs, Eddie?"

I shook my head. "I'm sorry, Larry. I've been having trouble sleeping, and I haven't been eating well enough, I guess."

He walked over near the window and took a deep breath. "Everybody's got problems," he said. "Everybody's got tough times. When I was nine years old in the Warsaw ghetto I was so hungry I ate a leather belt." He turned and faced me with a flourish.

I fought the impulse to smile or ask him how it tasted. It was my third time around on the belt story.

"You can be a big success on the show," he said. "And then, who knows? But you've gotta get it together. And by that I mean you gotta be here on time with your head on straight and ready to work. Will you do that?"

I stood up and shook his hand. "I appreciate your time. I'll try my best."

"That's not what I asked," he said, holding my gaze, and letting me know with his eyes that I was replaceable.

I looked at him, nodded respectfully, and excused myself.

12

We were sitting in a McDonald's on Eighth Avenue near Columbus Circle. Benjamin had in front of him a Big Mac, a Chicken McNuggets, two orders of french fries, and a large Coke. I was sipping on a cup of coffee and smoking a cigarette.

We had been to my mother's for lunch and then spent the rest of the afternoon touring a World War Two battleship that was docked at one of the piers on the Hudson River. Room after room of buttons and levers, Benjamin running around touching them all, and me trudging behind like a member of a chain gang. World War Two culture, in its many forms, had always bored me.

I felt a swell of emotion as I looked at Benjamin. Every time I saw him there were new mannerisms, new expressions, but also a growing distance between us. We hadn't lived together in almost three years, and though I would always love him, I was coming to realize that I would not always know him.

"Mommy doesn't love Aaron anymore," he said. He had a silly, nervous, seven-year-old smile on his face.

"How do you know?"

"She's been crying a lot."

"She always cried a lot," I said.

"And they've been arguing a lot. She comes home from work, she doesn't even kiss him. She goes right into the bedroom and shuts the door. Is that love?" He held up his hands for effect.

"Eat your hamburger."

Laura had married Aaron a little over a year ago. I'd met him a few times, and he seemed okay to me. A lawyer, good sense of humor, practical, with reasonable opinions about everything; the kind of boy my mama wanted me to be. I was hoping that Benjamin was wrong because I'd come to think of Aaron as the man to finish what I couldn't.

"How are you getting along with Aaron?"

He shrugged, and when he spoke I could see hamburger roll churn up and down in his mouth. "He's okay. He's got money."

"Living with you," I replied, "he better have money."

"Mommy called him a wimp."

"That doesn't sound like her."

"Oh, yeah? Well then who do you think I was hearing, Santa Claus?"

I noted Benjamin's sarcasm. It was a recent development, and I guessed it would grow and get more and more annoying until he was about fifteen or sixteen, at which point he would have other problems like drugs and pimples and girls.

"People can love each other," I said, without conviction, "and not get along all the time."

"Are you ever coming back?" he asked.

Every few months he asked me a question like this. It usually unnerved me, and he knew it. "Not to live," I said, "but you know I'm always there for you, right?"

He smiled. Benjamin has one of the all-time smiles. One

second his face will be composed, even thoughtful, and the next, all you can see are teeth and squinty eyes. "Daddy?" he asked.

"Yes?"

"Remember when you used to throw me way up in the air and I'd land in the bed and bounce up?"

"Yeah, I remember."

"Oh, man," he said to himself, savoring the memory, "that was great."

It was almost six o'clock now, and the place was getting noisy and crowded. As I watched Benjamin work on the end of his hamburger I was suddenly consumed by the idea that I would never see him again. Without thinking, I reached out and touched his cheek. He looked up at me and said, "Daddy, I love you."

"I love you," I replied, my voice cracking.

"Dad?"

"Yes?"

"There's this model spaceship at the drugstore. I've been thinking about getting it."

I stared at him, unable to speak.

"It costs fifteen ninety-nine."

I put my head on my folded arms and let the tears come silently. After a time I became dimly aware of a steady tapping on my arm, and I looked up into Benjamin's concerned face.

"Daddy," he said, "don't worry about the money for the spaceship. I can get it off of Aaron."

As soon as Laura opened the door to their apartment in the West Eighties, Benjamin wriggled inside, model spaceship firmly in hand, and disappeared.

Laura looked different. She had her red hair cut short, something she'd talked about doing for a long time, and she had it in sort of a wet look combed evenly back. I found the symmetry striking, and it made her facial features, the high cheekbones, the pale blue eyes, the long delicate nose, more distinct, almost regal. She was wearing a tight, white button-down shirt, a short blue skirt, and red high heels.

"You look great," I said.

"Oh, thanks," she said absently, blushing slightly. "Come on in—we'll have a drink."

I followed her down a long hardwood hallway that traversed the apartment. It dead-ended at the kitchen.

"Where's Aaron?" I asked.

She paused and then said, "He's at his mother's," and from her tone she might have added, "where he belongs." She stood with her back to me at the kitchen counter while she fixed our drinks, and as I watched her I felt a mild sexual stirring. I wondered idly what it would be like with her now, after three years. An interesting thought, I concluded, but a bad idea.

"I saw the show," she said, sitting down with the drinks. "It seems like a good part."

"Yeah, it's a good part, but I don't know how much longer I'll be doing it."

"Well," she said easily, "maybe they'll renew it."

"That's not what I mean."

She bent her head toward me. "What do you mean?"

I suddenly felt short of breath and a little dizzy. It was an effort to speak. "I've got some things to take care of. I don't like to sound mysterious, but it's not anything I can talk about yet."

She crinkled her nose and smiled at me. "What's the matter, did you get some girl pregnant?"

I tried, and failed, to smile back at her. "No, nothing like that."

She put her hand on mine and squeezed it softly. "I'm sorry, Eddie. Whatever it is, I'm sorry it had to happen now."

We sat sipping our drinks in silence, and I began to calm down again. I was about to say something dull about how nice the apartment looked when she said, "Aaron and I are splitting up."

"Oh," I said quietly.

She was leaning forward now, making imaginary designs with her index finger on the table, and at the angle she was sitting, most of her right breast was exposed through a fold of her shirt. I stared at it thoughtfully and said, "Should I be sorry?"

"I don't know," she said tiredly. "A mistake is a mistake. I'm more relieved than anything. I began to hate him so much it was scary. I mean, I kept thinking of all those forties movies where the wife is always killing the husband. Except I didn't even have a good motive—no big insurance policy, not even a lover, just disgust."

I took a deep breath. "That's too bad."

She waved her hand as if to negate the whole issue. "It's not too bad. I want to be alone for a while, maybe a long while. It seems to be the thing to do, I don't know." She paused and then looked up at me. "People can be so disappointing."

I raised my empty glass. "I'll drink to that."

She took the glass and went to refill it. "How about you?" she asked me. "Are you seeing anyone?"

"Sort of."

She came back with the drink, smiling. "Typical Eddie Black answer—equivocal and noncommittal."

"Is that the way you think of me?" I asked.

"I don't know what I think of you. I'm beginning to believe some of your sexual theories, though."

"I don't have any sexual theories."

"Yes you do, or you did. You used to say that marriage was a capitalist tool to keep people tied to the corporate state."

"Did I say that?"

She put her hand on my thigh and took it off. "Oh, come on. Remember we were in the Carmine Street apartment, and everybody used to come over and talk philosophy?"

I smiled and nodded in recollection. "Yes, I remember it. I remember it so well that everything since seems like a blur."

She leaned forward. "What do you mean?"

I shook my head in exasperation, as if the answer should have been obvious. "What I mean is that I cared about things then, I believed in things. I was stupid, and I was happy." I paused and looked at her. "I was even in love. Now? What the fuck? Whatever gives me a little more pleasure, whatever spares me some pain, that's where I go. That's all that's left of me."

Laura didn't answer right away; she seemed to be staring at a point above my head. "That's very sad," she said finally. Then her eyes met mine. "But I don't think it's true."

I felt the emotion come loose inside me, and I wanted to talk to her and to tell her things I hadn't even allowed myself to think. But the truth was so brutal, and her eyes were so gentle that when I started to speak my voice cracked and I just shook my head and turned away.

She touched my hand, and then got up and left the kitchen. I dimly heard her voice in the distance, and then Benjamin's, as I sipped on my drink and regained my composure.

Laura returned, smiling. "The spaceship is halfway built," she said. "He wants you to come and help him finish it."

I shook my head. I was never mechanically inclined.

"I know," she said, "I told him you wouldn't."

She made herself another drink, and we made small talk about business and family. Laura had always worked for her father—he owned a travel agency in Queens. He was about to retire, and she was taking over and moving the office into the city. It sounded like a rash move to me, but Laura's business sense was always a lot better than mine so I didn't say anything.

She sat back down at the table and looked at me speculatively. "When you said you were in love before, was that with me or was it with Stella?"

I frowned at her. "You know damn well who it was with. I didn't even like Stella."

"You liked her enough to sleep with her."

"That's right," I said angrily, holding my ground. "I liked her enough to sleep with her."

Laura looked up at the ceiling and laughed in a bittersweet way. "You two used to argue for hours. You were definitely the stars of the show. And the issues were always sex-related. I should have known all along, but I guess I didn't want to."

There was a long silence, and then I said, "It was strange. Stella was strange. There was something between us—intellectually—it had to be exorcised."

Laura looked at me ironically and then burst out laughing. I watched the color flood her face and thought how beautiful she was.

"Eddie," she said, "it doesn't matter anymore. But don't bring exorcism into it."

I leaned close to her. "If it doesn't matter anymore, then why are you bringing it up?"

She looked at me quickly, and, having no answer, she reverted to a childlike girlishness. " 'Cause I feel like it." In that instant, and in her expression, the smell of her, the sense of her came to me. My hand moved through her shirt and came to rest on her soft tit.

She turned her head slowly and looked me in the face. Her own face was filled partly with comedy and partly with a challenge, but then she looked past me and her eyes seemed to settle on something in the distance.

Instinctively, I looked behind me to the kitchen doorway. Benjamin was there, holding a piece of his model in his hand. He smiled at me conspiratorially.

"Daddy, are you sleeping over tonight?"

My hand slipped away from Laura and onto the table. "No," I replied, getting to my feet. "As a matter of fact I was just leaving."

13

It was ten o'clock on Friday night. I was lying back on the couch puffing intermittently on a joint that kept going out and sipping from a bottle of Bushmills.

In front of me on the coffee table were three objects: an ashtray, a Bible, and a .25 caliber semiautomatic pistol. The gun had been purchased that morning for seventy-five dollars from a guy named Oscar, who managed the parking lot across the street. It was the second pistol I'd ever owned. The first one was when Laura and I and Benjamin had an apartment on the Lower East Side. The place had been broken into a few times so I'd picked up a gun for protection. Laura had proceeded to nag me about it constantly until I had finally taken the thing apart and thrown it out.

I didn't really hear the sound of the buzzer until the second one came, and then I heard the first in a sort of replay. I made no move to answer it. The only one I would have cared to see was Charlotte, and I hadn't been able to reach her for three days. I had also tried, in the spirit of keeping one's enemies close, to reach Vincent, but he hadn't been around either. Both of these contributed to a prophetic feeling that events were conspiring against me.

The next sound I heard was the slow chug of the ascending elevator. I stood up, picked up the gun, and flipped off the safety. Then I went to the front door and stood to the side of it. The elevator door opened, and I listened to the footsteps getting louder. A man, certainly, but a bit heavy and slow-footed for either Vincent or Luis.

The knock was strong and authoritative, like a cop.

"Who is it?"

"Greenberg," came the response. "Open up."

I leaned over and looked through the peephole to see the pudgy, distorted face of the detective. I was more relieved than anything else. At least Greenberg wouldn't kill me—not all at once, anyhow.

"Just a second."

I put the gun in a coat pocket in my closet, but I didn't bother with the joint in the ashtray. Let him bust me for it, I thought. It would offer some comic relief and probably be a boon to my career.

I opened the door. Greenberg wore the sarcastic smile I was becoming used to, but he seemed different tonight— wired and excited, like he had something cooking.

"Don't like to answer your buzzer, do you?" he said, in a friendly way.

"Ever heard of a telephone?"

He smiled and then sort of looked me up and down. "You look better on TV."

"Thanks."

He brushed past me and into the apartment, as if he owned the place.

"Who's been smoking dope in here?" he asked.

I closed the door and walked toward him, not answering.

He found the joint in the ashtray and held it up. "I have to confiscate this," he said. A gold butane lighter appeared in his hand, and he began to inhale vigorously on the joint while I watched him curiously. When he'd smoked the joint down he took the roach and ate it.

"Well," he said, "aren't you going to offer me a drink?"

"Aren't you on duty?"

He shook his head and laughed, a wild excitement in his eyes. "I am definitely not on duty. I came here for some friendly conversation, that's all."

I got him a glass from the kitchen, and he sat in one of the folding chairs while I went back to the couch. We were positioned identically to our first meeting.

Greenberg shook his head, as if marveling at the vicissitudes of life. Then his eyes focused on mine.

"I misled you last time."

I looked at him and waited.

"I misled you as to my interest in Willie. My . . . relationship with him is a little more personal. I'm going to tell you a story."

"Does it have a happy ending?"

He took the question a lot more seriously than I'd intended it. "I don't know," he said, finally. "It's not over yet."

"I first met your uncle many years ago. My partner, Johnny Leonetti, and I did business with Willie for over a year." He paused and smiled at the memory. "It was my fourth year on the force, and I made more money in that year than I had in the first three combined. At that time Willie had his hands in all kinds of stuff, street stuff—"

"What's this got to do—"

"Shut up," said Greenberg quietly, but his eyes were ablaze. "Johnny got into a dispute with some of Willie's people over money, and we had a meeting. Your uncle never raised his voice, but Johnny was a hothead and he started yelling and name-calling; he said Willie was a kike who had money but no balls and that if he didn't make Johnny an equal partner in this particular operation, he, Johnny, was going to put him out of business." Greenberg smiled sadly and lighted a cigarette. "Johnny was a decent man. He was under a lot of pressure—he had problems with his wife, he drank, and he had his own gambling debts. But even with all that it was just a very stupid thing for him to do—very stupid. After that meeting we went out for a drink and that's the last I saw of him. A week later they found his legs stuffed into a garbage can down on Kenmare Street. Sometime after that they found another piece of him in the Brooklyn Navy Yard. They never found his head." Greenberg looked up at me as if suddenly remembering where he was. "Maybe you could ask your uncle where it is."

I struggled to control the trembling in my voice. "I told you, I don't speak to my uncle."

"What goes around comes around," continued Greenberg. "That's what my man Parker always says. I used to think it was a bunch of nigger nonsense, but that's before you came into my life." He reached deep into his coat pocket and pulled out the knife I had stabbed Frank with. "Murder weapon," he stated flatly. "I even found a little print on the edge of the handle."

In a quiet terror I stared at Greenberg's face and struggled to keep my composure.

"The wonders of routine police work," said Greenberg happily. "It's the kind of shit they teach in the academy but nobody ever does. When the guy was killed we couldn't find any witnesses. Well, we rechecked the neighborhood and found this lady lives in a place I thought was a cheese factory. She had a plane to catch which was why she wasn't there the first time around, but it's also why she remembered the exact time she saw you guys arguing with Frank on the loading dock—four thirty-five."

"That doesn't mean shit," I said. If there was conviction

in my voice, there was none in my heart. I was a fatally
wounded animal, still moving around on instinct.

"It means a lot more than shit," retorted Greenberg,
"but that's not all."

He leaned back in his seat—a dramatic pause before de-
livering the coup de grace.

"Vincent Minetta was arrested two days ago in Brooklyn
for assault and battery on his wife. He knocked her around
pretty good: two black eyes, a couple of broken ribs, teeth,
bruises all over."

I closed my eyes and shook my head. I thought painfully
of Julie, but not for long. I had my own problems.

"Is she going to be okay?" I asked.

He waved his hand. "Yeah, she'll be fine. But the interesting thing is Minetta's in jail on this wife-beating thing he
asks to speak with me. The guy's a fucking wreck, he hates
himself, but more important he ain't no fan of yours anymore
either. I don't know what went down with you two, and
frankly I don't care. He tells me you got into an argument
with Popowski about your paycheck. He tried to break it up
but you pulled the blade and put Frank away. All along I'm
thinking you're covering for him, and now I find it's the opposite. Life's a bitch, isn't it?"

I was no longer facing him, but staring at my lap. The
final vestiges of resistance had washed away, and I was already beginning to try to summon the dignity to accept my
fate. For Vincent, I felt not even a trace of bitterness. He had
snapped, but he'd had a good reason to. I looked at Greenberg calmly. "I want a lawyer."

"You don't need one," he replied.

"Why not?" I asked, annoyed.

"Because I don't intend to arrest you."

I stared at him and waited. A sick man, I thought, to
play games like this now. I considered jail: Did one get

fucked in the ass on the first day, or did they give you a few weeks to get acclimated? I saw myself at the age of, say, forty-five, soft, pasty-faced, sitting in a cell smoking a Lucky Strike. I'd probably be exceedingly well read, maybe even have some sort of intellectual project going. I had always liked reading German philosophy, and the poetry, too. In prison I could take the time to learn the language and become a real scholar. Or perhaps I'd be a religious fanatic—sit around all day citing passages from the Bible and debating Muslims.

"I don't intend to arrest you," repeated Greenberg, "because within two weeks you are going to pay me the grand sum of five hundred thousand dollars—in cash. When I get that, the case is closed."

His last four words, "the case is closed," sent an involuntary spark of something like hope through my chest, but this was quickly dashed. From where he was sitting, Greenberg could have spit the entire length of my apartment. Who did he think I was?

"I don't have that kind of money," I said.

"I know," he said, in a voice barely audible. "Not too many people do."

Slowly, I began to understand him, and even as I shook my head, he started to lay it out.

"The way I figure it," he said, "it's the only reasonable solution. Willie's good for that kind of bread, I know he is. It saves the life and the future," he gestured to me with his hand, "of a fine young man of considerable possibility. And last but not least, it will provide an early and suitably stylish retirement for a diligent public servant."

I stared at Greenberg's round, puffy face. I found it easy to visualize him at various points in his life: as a young man in his twenties, as a teenager, even as a small child.

"Give me a cigarette," I said to him. I lighted it and blew

some smoke toward the ceiling. "You're serious about this," I stated.

He nodded. "Never have I been so serious."

"How do I know you won't take the money and arrest me anyhow?"

He laughed shortly. "I wouldn't pull that on Willie. I want to be alive to spend the money."

I nodded. I still couldn't take this scheme in all seriousness, but my mind was starting to focus on it. "That might be a problem in any event."

For the first time, Greenberg showed a lack of confidence. He dropped his gaze for a moment and then returned it. "That's a risk I'm willing to take," he said.

"What about Vincent?" I asked. "What's to prevent him from going to another cop and telling the same story?"

"Let me worry about Vincent."

"What does that mean?"

"It means that Vincent's in line for a little commission from all this."

I let out a short, mirthless laugh and considered, just for a moment, asking Willie for half a million dollars.

"Forget it," I said. "I'll take my chances in court."

Greenberg snorted sarcastically. "You'll take your chances in court. If you get the best lawyer in the world, give as much as I'm asking to a judge, you'll still spend the next ten years in jail. And I'm being conservative. You killed a man, in the course of a robbery, no less. That's twenty-five to life automatically these days. And let me tell you another thing, let me give you the benefit of thirty-three years as a policeman." He pointed his index finger to his right temple. "You won't make it. Mentally, you won't make it. One, maybe two years, you could do, come out and put it behind you, but a long jail term?" He shook his head.

I couldn't have removed my eyes from Greenberg's face if I'd tried, and the pounding of my heart was like thunder. "What if he doesn't have it?" I asked weakly. "What if he just says no?"

"That's two questions," said Greenberg. "As to the first I can tell you that in nineteen fifty when me and Tommy protected his Manhattan gambling he had to net for himself over a million dollars. I was close enough to it that I can say that for sure. That's net cash for one operation in one year, and that's more than thirty years ago. Now he's into Vegas, he's into the Bahamas, and who knows what the fuck else where the fuck else. He lives like he owns a fucking shoe store, but he's rich enough that what I'm asking is chump change."

Greenberg was leaning forward intently. His eyes were shining, and there was a fine sweat on his forehead.

"What if he says no?" I whispered.

His expression became unsympathetic, and he rose heavily to his feet. When he was at the door he turned and shrugged philosophically. "I can't solve all your problems for you," he said. "After all, I'm not God."

I stayed on the couch for several minutes as my body quivered. My clothes suddenly felt suffocatingly tight, and I ripped my shirt off viciously, scattering buttons on the couch and floor.

I walked over to the desk and pulled out my new gun. I sniffed the metal, and then I rested it on the side of my face for a moment. It gave me some comfort to know that Greenberg was wrong in thinking I had only two choices. I had at least three.

14

I stopped to rest a moment and to gather myself. It had been almost fifteen years since I'd been here, and everything seemed smaller since those occasional Sunday afternoons when my mother and I would drive out to visit.

For the most part you could have exchanged this street with a thousand others in Queens and hardly have known the difference: rows of nearly identical red-brick two-family homes, with their small terraces and their neat front lawns. But on this street the symmetry was broken by an unusual construction in the middle of the block.

This house was larger than the others, taking up two lots instead of one, and the architectural style was more recent. The roof was in the shape of a triangle and perfectly flat. The masonry was beige, and a third of the front facade was a large picture window. In Scarsdale it wouldn't have drawn a second look, but in Rockaway the house was striking.

I walked up the front steps and onto a shaded patio filled with a variety of outdoor furniture and plants. I rang the doorbell, and a minute later I was face to face with a stout, elderly woman wearing a blue housedress.

"Yes?" she asked.

"Hello, Aunt Ethel. It's Eddie."

She froze for a second, then leaned forward and peered at me. When recognition came she tried to smile, but it was weak. Ethel had never been much of a hostess.

Still with the sickly, awkward smile on her face, she leaned over and kissed me on the cheek. "Come in, dear. I have some coffee."

I stepped into the house and said, "I'm sorry I didn't call first."

She looked at me quickly. "I hope nothing's wrong."

"Is Willie around?"

"He's upstairs taking a nap. Sit down. Have you had lunch yet?"

She went into the kitchen for a few minutes and returned with an egg salad sandwich and a cup of coffee. She was calmer now. She made mention of my role in "Hillsdale" and asked me a lot of questions about the family. I answered mechanically and showed her some pictures I had of Benjamin.

"So," she said, after a while, "to what do we owe the honor?"

"Oh," I replied casually, "I just have a few things to talk to Willie about, that's all."

"None of my business?" she asked cattily.

I averted my eyes and let my silence be her answer.

Ethel excused herself and went upstairs, presumably to wake him up. When she came down she didn't look at me or talk to me, but went into the kitchen and started tinkering around. A few minutes later I heard some shuffling and then the slow, heavy footsteps of my uncle descending the stairs. I rose out of my chair to meet him.

He walked right through my extended hand and hugged me, holding my head to his chest. Willie was the only member of my family who was taller than I was; he was about six foot four. He held me out by the shoulders as we looked at each other. He had a bit less hair and a few more wrinkles since I'd seen him last, but he didn't look that much different because the eyes, always his dominant feature, were still dominant. They were pale blue and very large, but the thing about them was that they didn't seem to have any definition. It was as if some blue paint had been carelessly thrown in there, and the effect was that Willie didn't look at you, he enveloped you.

I leaned forward slightly and whispered, "I need to speak to you."

"Okay," he said softly. "First we have a cup of coffee together, and then we go talk."

When we were seated he said, "I heard a rumor there's pictures of Benjamin here. Where are they?"

He looked at them intently, spending, it seemed to me, a long time on each one. Occasionally, a deep sound like a growl would come out of him; that was how he laughed. Ethel was with us for a while, but she couldn't seem to stay still. She kept getting up and going into the kitchen and coming back again. During one of her absences I spoke to Willie. "I'm in trouble. I have to talk to you alone."

He gave me a hard look, as if to tell me this better not be some kind of bullshit, but when I held his gaze he sighed philosophically and got out of his chair.

"Ethel," he said, pitching his voice into the kitchen, "we'll be downstairs—in the study."

Ethel came through the swinging door as if shot from a cannon. "Why are you going to the study?" she demanded.

"To talk," said Willie.

She looked at me suspiciously and said, "Who are you all of a sudden that you need so much privacy—Henry Kissinger?"

"That's enough, God damn it!" said Willie harshly. "You go into the kitchen," he said, pointing at Ethel. "And mind your own business."

I followed Willie through a hallway and then down a flight of stairs. We passed a den area with a television and a couch and went into his study. It was a large room, about twice the size of my own apartment, and in it was thick brown wall-to-wall carpeting, a huge mahogany desk, and a lot of leather furniture scattered around.

"A drink?" he asked. There was a distinct change in his tone now: he was sharper and more businesslike. I declined the drink.

He sat behind the desk and gestured for me to sit on the chair across from him. Then he gave me a long, appraising, and unsettling look.

"So," he said, a trace of amusement on his face, "what kind of trouble could you be in, a *pisher* like you? You get some girl pregnant?"

"I killed a man."

His head snapped back, as if from a blow, and his lips tightened. He seemed insulted. "What?"

I averted my eyes and exhaled.

"I take it," he said, "that this is not a joke."

I shook my head and said, "No joke."

I heard him sigh deeply, and when I looked at him he seemed tired and much older. "I'm not a priest," he said quietly, "or even a rabbi. I hope you haven't come to ask forgiveness."

No, I thought, I need a helluva lot more than forgiveness.

We stared at each other for a long moment. It seemed to me that Willie was trying to decide right then and there whether to involve himself at all or to invite me to leave.

"You better start from the beginning," he said finally. "And go slowly. I'm seventy-six years old."

I did as he asked. I told the story chronologically and simply, for I had prepared for this as I would have for a scene in a play. The only thing I consciously omitted was my night with Julie. I couldn't see that it meant anything now, plus I knew Willie to be straitlaced on sexual matters.

He kept his eyes closed as I spoke. If he remembered Greenberg or Johnny Leonetti, he didn't show it, though when I got to Greenberg's financial "offer" Willie's eyebrows raised slightly. A minute or so after I'd stopped talking he opened his eyes and stared at the ceiling. "This upsets me very much," he said.

What about the money? I asked silently. But what I said was, "Do you think you can help?"

He must have read my mind because he fixed me with a vicious glare and said, "It will be a cold day in Hell before I pay that kind of money to a New York City police detective."

Despite his words, I felt a spark of hope, for it seemed that Willie had made my problem his problem. Again, he must have read my mind.

"I make no promises," he said flatly. "I have certain resources, but I'm not a miracle worker. This is already pretty far gone, and it's sloppy. Greenberg knows you did it, this fellow Vincent knows you did it, that's two people too many, and you can bet that's not all. Also, it could be a setup to nail me on some kind of bribery charge."

"I think Greenberg wants the money for himself," I said.

"You think, you think," retorted Willie sarcastically.

"You should have thought before you picked up that knife. You should have thought ten years ago when you turned down a college scholarship and went to drama school. You had an IQ of a hundred and forty, your mother told me, and look at you."

Despite the haplessness of my position, I was in no mood for a lecture. "I happen to be employed at the moment, in case you haven't noticed."

He waved his hand in annoyance. "I saw you on the television. That *fachokta* nonsense doesn't impress me. Your cousin Peter, there's a boy, happens to have a very good job with Salomon Brothers."

"Fuck Peter. That guy is an asshole."

"Fuck Peter Asshole went to college, then he went to business school, and his mother told Ethel he makes about a hundred thousand dollars a year already."

"That's not as much as you make," I said evenly. "And you never even finished high school."

Willie's eyes narrowed, and he paled slightly. "I grew up in a cesspool," he said quietly. "That's why I smell like shit. What's your excuse?"

I stood up and faced him. "I don't have any excuses." I turned and started for the door. "I'm just sorry I came here."

"Sit down!"

I hesitated and looked back at him. I was going to leave anyway, but his eyes seemed first to paralyze me and then to return my body to the chair.

After a silence, he said, "You have your own mind, you always did. I respect that. In fact, I'm sorry that I mentioned Peter, because to tell you the truth, I never liked that little tight-ass. But sometimes they're the ones with the easier time of it."

"What should I do?"

"Sit still for a few days," he replied. "I'll have someone talk to this shyster, and we'll see what's what."

"If it comes down to money," I said, "I might be able to pay you back sometime."

Willie grunted. "And I might win the Nobel Peace Prize. Let's deal in reality for the moment.

"Besides," he continued, "the money's not the only issue. He picked out a number. It's a negotiating position, and that's okay. The main thing is, will it work, and I have doubts about that. It's so sloppy. You might do better to face the charges. I'd rather spend my money on a judge."

"Greenberg says it'll be twenty-five to life."

"Stop getting your legal advice from Greenberg. There are lots of possibilities, but I don't want to talk about that now. Go upstairs, say goodbye to my wife, and I'll be in touch with you."

We stood up together, and he walked me to the door. "I'm scared, Willie," I told him.

He patted me on the back. "I don't blame you."

15

It was a cool, sharp autumn night, and as I stood on the corner outside the studio it seemed to me that the faces of the hurried people on the street matched the weather. Everyone seemed to move faster now and with purpose.

Since my visit to Willie almost a week ago I had heard nothing from him. I had shot three more very smooth episodes of "Hillsdale," the last of which had catapulted me from villain to a romantic lead. Next week Dolores and I were to have dinner with the producer, who was going to offer me a one-year contract. Dolores said they would offer sixty thousand dollars, but she would try for eighty. I was just hoping I could be there. It was the sort of victory I used to dream of, and the hollowness I felt now that it had come served to produce an amused kind of irony in my attitude. Even the thought of being arrested did not seem to weigh heavily at the moment. Part of it was Willie, but part of it was that I had lived long enough now with the idea that I was too tired to fight it. This was America; you win big, you lose big, you die early, fuck it.

But then there was Charlotte. It had been over a month, and I still hadn't been able to reach her. One night the line had been busy for hours and then nothing. I had gone by her apartment twice, still with no luck. Had I lost her? The thought of it was scarier and more painful than I cared to admit.

I hopped a cab down to the Village and stopped for a drink in one of the bars near Sheridan Square. It was Friday night, and the place was already crowded with trendy-looking people. A blond woman of about twenty came over and asked me if I was Eddie Black. I told her I was and we talked politely for a minute or two. When she left, I went to the pay phone in the back and dialed Charlotte's number. A surge of anticipation went through me at the sound of the busy signal. She lived only two blocks away so I hung up the phone, paid for my drink, and left the bar.

I was a little nervous walking to her place. I had already considered that she might want to end it with me. It didn't feel right, but Charlotte was not a woman I felt I understood, much less could predict. The way she would look at me with that preoccupied but intense expression—what was she thinking? I tried to envision her telling me to walk. She would be eloquent, though not verbose, cool, but not detached. And I would remain composed, but it would be the phony composure of the reeling boxer who smiles and shakes his head while his knees vibrate just before the knockout.

She lived on one of those crooked little streets between Sixth and Seventh avenues near West Fourth. She had the basement apartment in a brownstone with her entrance to the side and down a few steps. There was a black iron gate there with a clean white buzzer on it.

I pressed the buzzer three times before I heard the front door click open, but the voice that asked "Who is it?" was not Charlotte's, but another woman's.

"It's Eddie," I replied. "I'm looking for Charlotte."

"She's not here," replied the now unfriendly voice. "She doesn't live here anymore."

"Oh, really? Where does she live?"

My answer to that was the sound of the door slamming shut.

I cursed silently, put my finger on the buzzer, and kept it there. It was at least three minutes later that the door opened again, this time all the way so that I got a partial look through the bars at a slim woman of about forty with wild grayish hair.

"Are you Margaret?" I asked.

"Yes, and I wish you would leave."

"I'm not leaving. And if you don't let me in I'm going to climb over this gate and kick the fucking door down."

She let out a sarcastic sort of grunt and said, "Well, if it isn't John Wayne himself." She disappeared into the house, and a second later the gate buzzer went off, and I went down the steps and into the apartment.

I'd stayed over here a couple of times, but the place was unrecognizable to me now. There were cardboard boxes, some filled, some empty, lying all over the place. And no furniture left except a small kitchen table and chairs in the back. Margaret was in one of the rooms packing a box and ignoring me completely.

I watched her for a moment. She was tall and very slender, but her body did not suggest anything fragile. Charlotte had told me that Margaret was a serious bicyclist, had entered races in Europe years ago, and even under her baggy jeans I could sense the power in her legs. Despite nice blue-gray eyes, her face was too hard-bitten to rightly be called pretty, but there was plenty of appeal there, and I could easily see them together. A handsome couple, even.

"What's going on?" I asked.

With a deep breath, she stopped what she was doing and faced me. Her expression would have been contemptuous had it not been so impersonal.

"Charlotte said that if you came by I should tell you that she's going away. She doesn't want to talk to you or see you now. When she gets back she might call you, but she doesn't know when that will be."

Not having a ready reply, I sauntered back to the kitchen. There was a bottle of gin and some cigarettes on the table. I sat down, lighted a cigarette, and poured myself a drink. After a few minutes I walked back into the room where Margaret was and leaned against the wall.

"She's in Vermont, isn't she?" I said, in more of a statement than a question. And from her hesitation I figured I was probably right. "I think I'll rent a car and go see her."

"Don't do that," she said quickly, fear in her face. She walked up closer to me, and though it could have been my imagination, her expression seemed just a shade sympathetic. "Look," she said, "I can't make it any clearer. She really doesn't want to see you. You're just gonna have to accept it."

"Please," I replied icily, "don't tell me what I have to accept."

Now there was nothing ambiguous about the emotion on her face: it was bald hatred. "The original macho man!" she spat. "Well, let me tell you why she will never speak to you again. Last week someone rang the doorbell, said he was a friend of yours and had a message from you. You know what that message was?"

My chest was constricted, and I could feel a hotness behind my eyes. "What was the message?" I whispered.

"He raped her!"

Even as I shook my head I could feel a sickening elec-

tricity go from my belly to my mouth and escape with dizzy-
ing power. "No," I said. "No . . ."

"You fucking bastard!" screamed Margaret, and the
tears sprang from her eyes, and she started hitting me on my
face and chest. In an anguished sort of daze, I took the blows
for a minute, and then I grabbed her arms.

"Who?" I asked.

She shook her head. "I don't know who."

I led her back to the kitchen and sat her down at the
table. My whole body was trembling, and my words seemed
to come out hours after I'd formed them.

"What did the police say?"

Margaret was still out of control, and I grabbed her head
and made her look at me. "You gotta talk to me, Margaret.
You gotta talk to me."

She stopped sobbing and nodded her head miserably.

"What did the police say?"

"She wouldn't call the police. I begged her to, but she
was adamant."

"Did she tell you what he looked like?"

"Just that he had a mustache and he was skinny and
disgusting. He had a knife . . ."

"He was Puerto Rican," I said quietly.

She looked at me sharply and said, "Yes, he was Puerto
Rican. He had her there for three hours. Three hours. She
has a scar from here," Margaret put her finger at the bottom
of her neck and ran it down to the bottom of her belly, "to
here. He said he saw it in a movie once and wanted to try it
out."

I leaned back in the chair as an involuntary groan
escaped my lips. I closed my eyes and wave after wave of horror ran through me. I heard Margaret get up and then water
running from the bathroom. I listened intently to the sound

in a desperate attempt to focus on something, so as not to lose myself in the storm inside me.

Margaret came back. She was red-eyed but composed. "You don't look so good," she said. She poured me a drink, and I gulped it down.

"Charlotte's going to survive," she said calmly. "It was real bad the first few days, she just lay in bed, she wouldn't talk or eat or anything, but she's up and around now; a little shell-shocked, but we're going away next week to Australia and she's actually looking forward to it."

I nodded, feeling my faculties begin to come back, but still unable to speak.

"Sometimes," continued Margaret, "I think it's worse for me. She went through it, it happened to her, but with me it's all these images of what it must have been like, and they keep coming. I haven't been able to sleep more than two hours at a time since it happened.

"And the guy," she continued bitterly. "He's still out there. It makes me sick." She looked at me for a long moment. "You know who it is, don't you?"

When I didn't answer, she said, "It doesn't matter, that's the bitch of it. Charlotte won't go to the police, she won't identify the guy. There's nothing we can do."

I was staring at her, tapping my index finger against my lip. "Margaret, are you going to tell her that I know?"

She hesitated and then said, "I'm not sure. I don't think very soon."

"If you ever do, tell her that I'm sorry."

She nodded, and for that moment Charlotte's presence was at the table with us. I took Margaret's hand in mine and kissed it. Then I got to my feet and left the apartment.

I walked home through Washington Square Park, and though I didn't intend it, I found myself standing by the sandbox where Charlotte and I had made love. She's still alive, I thought gratefully, and then I closed my eyes and tried to feel her terror, her humiliation, in the hope that it might somehow lessen her own burden.

When I got home I took a shower and sat on the edge of my bed. I lifted the telephone receiver off its hook and dialed a number.

It was a tired voice at the other end that said, "Hello."

"Aunt Ethel, it's Eddie. Is Willie there?"

"No, he isn't, dear. He'll be back tomorrow afternoon. He doesn't talk on the telephone anyway, you know that."

I hesitated for a moment, and then I said, "Can I leave a message?"

"Certainly," she replied. "If it's not too long. I'm in bed, and I don't have a pencil."

"All bets are off."

"What?" she said quickly. "I can't hear you. What's the message?"

I closed my eyes as I felt a surging wave of grief rise in me. "Never mind," I whispered to the telephone. "It's not important."

16

At seven o'clock the next morning, Saturday, I was standing on the corner of Broadway and Eighth Street, dressed in jeans, sneakers, and a long, gray, army-style raincoat. As I raised my arm to hail the noisy, creaking Checker cab, I had the strange sensation of having multiplied and of watching my own every movement.

Twenty-five miles later I was standing in front of the information desk at Brooklyn Jewish Hospital. Discovering Julie's location was simple enough, but getting to her was another matter: visiting hours didn't start until eleven. I was politely insistent to a middle-aged Nurse Kane, in charge of the floor, but it would have been for nought had the woman not recognized me from television.

After flatly denying my request to see Julie, she looked at me intently, snapped her fingers, and said, " 'Edge of Night'!"

I shook my head. " 'Hillsdale.' "

"Right!" she said, beaming. "The doctor, the psychiatrist. You're him."

I smiled uncomfortably and nodded.

She grabbed on to the side of my coat near the elbow and leaned closer to me. "Tell me something. Are you going to marry that heiress?"

I looked at her speculatively. The truth was that I had no idea what was going to happen on the show. I sighed and shrugged helplessly. "I'm not supposed to tell. We have our rules, too, Nurse Kane."

She backed up and folded her arms primly—ready to deal. "Perhaps," she said, "if I bend a rule, you'll bend a rule."

"We do marry," I said briskly. "Her father's against it, but he has a stroke and dies."

"What about the sister?" she demanded. "How do you handle her?"

"Oh, you mean Emily?" I asked, stalling for time.

"I don't remember her name," said Nurse Kane with annoyance. "She's only got one, right?"

"Yeah. Blackmail. Emily had an incestuous relationship with her father. I, Dr. Stone, can prove it."

She nodded seriously, as if this not only made sense, it was inevitable. "Last bed on the right," she said. "Room Six."

There were seven or eight other patients in Room Six, and each bed space was curtained off by two sheets hanging from a metal rod. Julie was sleeping when I got there, and I took a moment to look at her. Her left eye was swollen and discolored, and she wore a metal brace around her neck. I sat down on a stool beside the bed and touched her hand. Her eyes flipped open, and a second later she smiled. "Eddie," she said and squeezed my hand.

"Sorry to wake you," I said softly.

She gingerly propped herself up on some pillows and looked at me. The sleep was already gone from her eyes, and she seemed fine except that the neck brace didn't allow for much head movement. "I'm glad you came," she said. "I'm feeling good. I get out tomorrow."

I nodded and then said, "I'm sorry, Julie."

Her eyes clouded uncomfortably. "It's not your fault," she said. "It's not your fault. It had to do with me and Vincent."

I nodded again and averted my eyes.

"He had a nervous breakdown, Eddie," she continued. "He wasn't himself. He feels bad about what he told the police about you, but he says now that it's all going to work out. He's happy about that."

I leaned forward and touched her lightly on the cheek. "Julie, I need a favor."

"Sure," she said. "Anything."

"Luis," and the mention of his name caused a very slight, involuntary shudder in my chest. "I need to get in touch with him."

She looked at me quizzically, and then her face began to color. "You don't want to get in touch with him," she said. "Stay away from him."

"Where does he live?"

"Eddie," she said, her voice cracking. "What's going on?"

I took a deep breath and stood up. For the first time I became aware of that unattractive hospital odor, and I wanted to get out of there. Outside the room, in the hallway, Nurse Kane walked by with another, younger, nurse, and they both smiled at me.

I abruptly sat down, not on the stool this time, but on the edge of the bed. I took Julie's hand in mine and put my face within a few inches of hers.

"Luis was following me," I whispered. "You know that, right?"

She nodded.

"I was seeing a woman during that time. He must have followed me there one night because he went there again, and you know what he did?"

"What?" said Julie, in a trancelike whisper.

I leaned even closer and said the word slowly, "Rape. He raped her, and he cut her up with his knife."

The tiniest of shrieks escaped Julie's lips, and the color drained from her face.

"Where does he live?"

"Oh, Eddie."

"Where does he live?"

"I don't know."

I exhaled deeply and closed my eyes.

"But I know where he works," whispered Julie.

Slowly, I opened my eyes and gazed at her. Her expression was equal parts fear and hatred.

"He sells his dope in the city," she began mechanically. "West Fifty-sixth Street between Tenth and Eleventh avenues. I've been there. It's an abandoned building, red brick. All the windows are boarded up, except on the second floor. Saturday is his big day."

I moved to leave, but she grabbed my arm hard, almost digging her nails into my flesh. "He did it on his own, Eddie. Vincent didn't know about it. You've gotta believe that."

I took her hand off my arm and pressed it to my lips. Then I told her a half-truth: "I believe it."

In the hallway, Nurse Kane and her friend were waiting for me. Something in my face must have discouraged them because, in unison, they averted their eyes and walked quickly in the opposite direction.

17

I sat in the last seat at the counter of the doughnut shop and swirled the now cold coffee around in my mouth. There were all kinds of sparks and palpitations having their way in my stomach as I stared across Tenth Avenue and onto Fifty-sixth Street at the front of Luis's building.

It was still early, and very little was happening on the street. Some traffic on Tenth Avenue, a smattering of pedestrians, and a middle-aged bum sprawled in front and to the side of the abandoned red-brick tenement building.

I'd been there nearly a half-hour when a gray Mercedes convertible with New Jersey plates pulled up in front of the building, double-parked, and two skinny punker types, no more than eighteen years old, emerged from the car. They looked around the block in a parody of cool and then went inside. I took a deep breath and exhaled. No lock on the front door.

I reached into my pocket and took out a cigarette. I could hear my own breathing, like thunder, but the hand that held the match was so steady that I had to look at it for a second and wonder if it was really mine. I smoked the cigarette deliberately, and when I had smoked it down and then put it out in the ashtray I blew the final smoke out of my mouth toward the window and watched, as if in a dream, the front door of the building open, the two kids walk out, and then a third figure.

Luis, dressed in a red warm-up jacket and purple Converse sneakers, was doing the talking. He was moving his hands and smiling confidently, as if telling a funny story. The kids were standing in awkward poses, nodding obediently and smiling in all the right places. There was some soul-brother handshaking, and the kids went to their car. They looked around the street in the same ridiculous way they had on arriving and drove off.

Luis stood for a moment on the sidewalk. The bum yelled something to him in a deep, froggy voice, and he smiled, walked over to the bum, and threw some money down on the ground. Ah, Luis, I thought, as an exquisite rush of heat rose in my belly, even you have your contradictions.

He started back inside but hesitated on the front steps and started walking quickly down the street in the opposite direction and out of my sight. I walked outside and across Fifty-sixth Street in time to see him disappear into a little bodega near Eleventh Avenue.

I stood on the corner for a moment and shivered in the autumn chill. Then I moved across Tenth Avenue, feeling as if I had never walked before and afraid I might fall down. I pushed open the front door and stepped into a vestibule that stunk of urine and booze. As the door closed behind me and I looked at the ugly walls and the broken-down staircase, my heart began to pound painfully, and I had the impulse to flee. I even turned my body toward the door, and maybe I would have opened it and run out except that I couldn't imagine where I would go.

To my immediate right, just inside the door, was an

open space. It must have been a storage area at one time, but now it was bare. It extended under the stairwell on one side, and the other corner was parallel to the front door and so hidden from view that you would have to have been at least halfway up the first flight of stairs to have seen me.

I leaned against the wall and removed the pistol from my coat pocket. I held the gun awkwardly in my left hand while I wiped the moisture from my right. Then I flipped the safety off and waited. I breathed through my mouth in short, quick, quiet little gasps. Level with my eyes on the opposite wall was a simple piece of graffiti—"Sherry Fucks." I stared at it, at first just as a formation of letters, then wishing it would go away, then trying to imagine Sherry, fucking, and finally again as a shape without meaning.

There was laughter from just outside the door, followed by the froggy voice of the bum, and then Luis said, "You a crazy motherfucker." The door opened and the smell, the feel, the sense of him was near me. I whirled out of my corner, gun extended, and as his quizzical face turned toward me, as if in slow motion, I squeezed the trigger.

The sound was loud in the small space, but not deafening. Luis did a lightning three-sixty-degree turn but remained standing, and for a second I thought I had missed him entirely, but then I saw the blood begin to trickle down the right side of his neck. A sound came from his mouth, something like "oh" or "hey" in a high-pitched squeal, and I was reminded of the way people talk in comic strips. I fired again, and this time he bounced back directly against the wall and slumped down. He held his right hand high on the left side of his chest as if about to recite the Pledge of Allegiance. When was the last time this motherfucker said the Pledge of Allegiance? He looked up at me in a helpless and scared sort of wonder, and he started talking some kind of

shit, but I couldn't hear the words because I was nearly overcome by how easy this was once you got going.

There was more blood now, but then he started to move,
using his left arm to sort of crawl sideways up the steps. I
watched him for a moment, and then I stepped forward and
extended the gun.

"Stop!"

He stopped and looked at me like a child or a dog, but
when he spoke it was almost like an order. "Don't kill me,
man."

"Was she good?" I asked.

"You're crazy, man. Don't kill me."

"Was she good?" I repeated, louder.

He wouldn't answer. He wanted only to say what would
save his life so, in order to reassure him, I said, "I'm not
going to kill you. I just want to know if she was good."

There was hope in his eyes, and he was thinking, but he
still didn't know the answer so I had to spell it out.

"Tell me she was good, Luis. Tell me she was good."

"She was good," he said quickly. "She was great."

A moan of sweet malevolence escaped my lips, but as I
moved forward to put the barrel against his face, or perhaps
in his mouth, since I saw that in a movie once, the front door
swung open behind me and slammed into the side of my
body and face with enough force to knock me into the railing
and send me sprawling on the floor. When I looked up it
was into the barrel of another, much larger, gun than
my own.

"Drop it!" said the voice behind the gun, and though I
followed his order automatically there was something familiar, so I raised my eyes to look into his face.

The man was wearing a blue winter ski hat, the kind
that covers the face with openings for the eyes, nose, and

mouth. It didn't stop me from recognizing him, nor did it stop Luis.

"Vinny," said Luis desperately, "shoot the mother-fucker. Kill him!"

But Vincent was looking at me, and he wasn't moving, so Luis got on his knees and reached toward him. "Gimme the piece, man. Gimme the piece."

Vincent's head moved slowly away from me, and the hand that held the gun also moved away and then lowered almost casually to Luis's head.

"You scumbag," he said, and the gun spoke deafeningly, exploding Luis into a crimson oblivion.

18

"I didn't know about it," said Vincent. "He did it on his own. First I heard about it was when Julie called me this morning."

I sat beside him in the front seat of his taxicab. We were in the parking lot near Canal Street, the same gravel parking lot we used to use when we worked for Frank. The three Popowski trucks were still there, in fact, grimy and silent, sitting in a row. I wondered if trucks were capable of mourning.

"Sure I had him follow you," said Vincent. "I was nervous, and he owed me a favor. Remember that armed robbery thing I went up on? Well, I took the rap on that. I did it with Luis and another guy. They got me, but I didn't give up any names. Luis was always into this private-eye shit—he used to read the magazines, he even tried to get a license once so I asked him to spy on you because I thought . . . I don't know what I thought, but I didn't know about no rape. I don't go for that shit."

I stared across the river to New Jersey. The gunshots still echoed in my ears, but I thought of Charlotte. I pictured her in Vermont with Margaret, preparing for her trip, and I felt unspeakably sad.

"Greenberg tells me the deal with your uncle is going to go down pretty smooth," said Vincent.

I turned to look at him. He seemed nervous and uncomfortable. "It's amazing," he said, smiling awkwardly, "but I think it's going to work out for all of us. Things tend to work out, you know?"

"Do they?" I asked.

"Yeah, I think they do."

I stared at him for a long moment. "I gotta go, Vincent." My voice was barely audible.

When I got out of the cab, Vincent got out, too. "I can drop you off, man."

I shook my head. "That's okay."

"Eddie," he said, a faint note of pleading in his voice. "I was there for you, man, wasn't I?"

I was going to turn and leave, but the pain in Vincent's eyes held me there. "Yeah," I said finally. "You were there for me."

I reached over the hood of the car, and we touched hands. "Take care of yourself, Vincent."

"You too, Eddie."

19

The automobile looked out of place enough in front of my apartment that I stopped on the sidewalk to look at it. A sparkling silver Mercedes, the long kind, with tinted windows.

A dark-haired man in a camel's hair coat got out of the driver's side and looked straight at me. His expression was businesslike but friendly. He walked around the car and toward me.

"Eddie," he said, extending his hand, "I'm Joe Petrone." Joe Petrone was well into his forties, yet the skin on his face was absolutely flawless. He gestured back to the car with his eyes. "Your uncle would like to talk to you."

As I followed him to the car the air in my stomach seemed to rush out of me, and for a moment I thought I might black out. But this passed quickly and was replaced by a hollow kind of fear.

Willie was in the front seat. He turned his head halfway toward me, nodded, and grunted a hello. When Joe Petrone had settled in at the wheel he looked at Willie expectantly. Willie sighed and pitched his voice back to me.

"Is that place on Second Avenue—Ratner's—is that still open?"

"No," I replied. "It's closed."

He sighed again and waved his hand at the road. "Let's just drive around, Joe."

The car whispered forward and Willie said, "Greenberg got paid this morning. Three hundred grand." There was a pause, and then he added, with irony, "A negotiated settlement."

I exhaled and closed my eyes. "I guess that's good."

"Good for him," said Willie. "And good for you."

I stared at the wispy white hair on the back of Willie's head and wondered what to say. "Thank you" didn't seem appropriate.

"Don't tell anyone about this. Ever."

"Don't worry," I said, clearing my throat at the same time and garbling the words.

He moved uncomfortably in his seat and then spoke wistfully, as if to himself. "I did it for your mother and for the memory of your father."

I leaned back in my seat and half listened to Willie talk about the neighborhood, how it used to be, and how fucked up it was now. He pointed to a building on First Avenue and said something about a card room he used to have there fifty years ago.

The feeling of relief that was beginning to flood through me was tempered by a sense that there was more to say. I didn't know what, or by whom, but it turned out my instinct was right.

Willie grumbled something to Joe about heading back and then spoke to me. "There's one more thing."

"Yeah?"

"This guy Vince," said Willie. "He didn't make it."

"What do you mean he didn't make it?" I asked automatically.

"Greenberg said he was unstable," said Willie briskly. "He couldn't be trusted, and he knew everything."

I cursed softly as my insides began to tremble, and I reached for a cigarette.

"That's the way it is sometimes," said Willie. "One man's profit is another man's loss."

I lighted the cigarette, took a drag, and then crushed it in my hand, squeezing harder as the heat burned into me. "This is ugly," I said.

Both Willie and Joe Petrone turned in unison to look at me. Then they turned back again, and there was silence.

"Ugly," said Willie a minute later. "You shoulda' seen Joe over here before he got his face operation. That was ugly."

Joe Petrone snorted and grinned good-naturedly. Willie turned in his seat and looked at me. "You bet it's ugly," he seethed. "You think I need this shit?"

I watched him for a moment, and then I shook my head and closed my eyes.

"Look at me!" said Willie.

"I don't want to look at you."

"Then listen," he snapped. "If this comes back to me through you, nephew or not, you'll wish you were never born."

I looked up into his blue eyes. Willie Blue Eyes. I quivered inwardly at the malevolence that was all around us. "Too late," I said softly. "That's the way I feel now."

He broke his gaze and turned around. I stared out the window at two bums sprawled in a doorway. "How was he killed?" I whispered.

There was no answer for a few seconds, and then Willie

looked at Joe, and Joe looked at me. "He jumped out the window of his apartment," said Joe. "Suicide."

"Suicide," I repeated, as if it was the most normal thing. "That's nice."

"You'll get over this," said Willie. "You're free, and you have the advantage of youth."

"That's true," I said. "I have all the advantages."

"That's right," said Willie seriously. "Everything is ahead of you."

I moaned and leaned back on the seat, resting my head on the soft cushion.

A minute later I was back on the sidewalk in front of my apartment. Willie's window came down, and he looked at me impassively. "You're on your own," he said. "No more favors."

I stared back at him, wanting to speak but unable to. He seemed to understand, and his face softened. He started to say something himself, but cut it off and turned away. The window went up, and I watched the Mercedes float lazily down the block.

20

It was dark by the time I pulled the rented Chevy Impala onto the long dirt-and-gravel road that led to Charlotte's house in Vermont.

I hadn't been able to stay in the apartment for more than a few minutes after Willie had left so I had gone outside and walked in search of exhaustion, but in the end it was the city itself that was closing in on me.

And it hadn't been until I saw the first Albany sign on the thruway that I'd realized where I was going. Charlotte's presence had come to me with the force of a revelation. She was the answer to the pain, the horror, the awful freedom, and in her image it all even seemed to make sense.

As I drove slowly down the dark road amid the chattering of the crickets, I had my first feelings of apprehension. Would Charlotte even see me? She probably hated me now, blaming me, and perhaps rightly so, for the terrible violence done to her. And what about Margaret? Get out of here, I told myself. Let her get on with her own life.

But when I got to the end of the road I pulled to the side and turned off the ignition and the lights. The house itself offered an uncertain message. It was completely dark except for one faint light coming from what I guessed was the den downstairs. There was a Volkswagen bus parked in the driveway. I sat there for a long time, continuing to think of all the reasons I should leave, yet I felt powerless to do so. Where would I go? And who would I go to? All I wanted was a few words, a few minutes alone with her.

The sound of my feet crunching on the crisp ground was loud in my ears as I walked across the yard toward the front door. As I neared the house I could hear the faint sound of music; it sounded like Billie Holiday, and it was coming from the same place as the light. Now I had an even stronger sense that this was wrong, that this was a violation. I started to turn back toward the car, but stopped still in the middle of the yard.

The night was awesome. I listened to the now steady hum of the crickets, and I looked up into a full moon and a host of stars. What should I do, I asked silently, but there was no answer. I took a deep breath and turned around once again, but this time I walked not to the front door, but directly toward the light and the music. The window was at ground level; I went to the side of the house, slipped inside some bushes, and kneeled.

A fire was going in the fireplace, and I thought I saw a human figure in silhouette lying on its side in front of the couch.

Suddenly it moved, it rolled across the carpet, and Charlotte's naked body appeared next to the fire. I held my breath as she casually reached for one of the implements near the fireplace, and, still lying on her side, her body outstretched like some divine animal, stoked the fire.

She laid the implement back in place and then sprawled on her back and basked in the heat. I wanted to cry out, in hunger, in need, in sheer appreciation of her, and I might have, had it not been for another movement from the darkness. On her hands and knees and also naked, Margaret crawled into view. She moved around Charlotte in a circle a few times and for the first time I noticed the thin scar running down Charlotte's chest and belly. There was soft laughter, some kind of game, and then Margaret lowered her head and began to kiss Charlotte, first on the neck and the breasts and then down her belly to her thighs. I could hear soft moaning, their voices mingling as one as Charlotte's body began to move. In a trancelike state, and with tears streaming down my face, I watched Margaret make love to Charlotte's body as if conducting a symphony. At times with an almost methodical intensity causing her to cry out and move wildly, and then carelessly retreating, playing with her, and the sounds of their love came to me also like music so that I closed my eyes and listened until Charlotte's cries became louder and louder, not to be denied this time, and I had to wipe the tears from my eyes to see them again. To see them wrapped in each other's arms and rolling playfully in and out of the light of the fire.

I reeled back in the dirt and lay there for a moment trying to catch my breath. Then I crawled through the bushes and made my way back to the car.

21

It was just past midnight when I pulled into the parking lot of Dairy Maid, a large, glass-enclosed hamburger and ice cream place in the Bronx, near Van Cortlandt Park. I lighted a cigarette and stared inside for a few moments. There were three or four customers, a young woman in uniform behind the counter, and a tall, robustly built white-haired man of about sixty—a man I remembered well—Mr. Papakakis, the owner of Dairy Maid.

Papakakis looked a little older, but probably no less tough than he was when I used to hang out here more than ten years ago. We would congregate in the parking lot, ten of us, sometimes thirty of us, drinking, taking drugs, fighting, and generally serving as contrast to the blandness of the neighborhood. Our relationship to Papakakis was predictably strained. We spent almost no money inside, and we made trouble for him outside. What saved things from getting completely out of hand was that Papakakis could handle any five of us at once, and his bearing was such that he rarely had to prove it.

The last time I'd been here was a summer night after

my junior year in high school. I remembered the incident
clearly: a fight with some guys from Yonkers. Outnumbering
them two to one, our usual strategy, we'd taken care of
things easily, and when they were leaving in their car I had
thrown a rock that missed and shattered the glass of the front
door of Dairy Maid. Before I could run or really know what
had happened, I'd found myself jacked up against a car, Papakakis's maniacally enraged face against mine, and his
words came vividly back to me now. "I'm going to kill you,
you skinny little punk."

He hadn't killed me, only slapped me around some, and
then banished me from the premises of Dairy Maid for life. I
realized as I sat in the car that, technically speaking, that life
sentence was still in effect. Nonetheless, I got out, went inside, and took a seat at the counter. Papakakis was behind
the counter with his back to me, cleaning one of the machines. The uniformed girl came over to take my order. She
was a pretty, nervous-looking redhead, and she wore a name
tag that said "Louise."

"Hamburger and fries," I said.

"Grill's closed," said Papakakis, not even looking up.
"Hot dogs or ice cream, that's it."

Same old hard-ass, I thought, without malice. But just
the sound of his voice took me back and made me feel comfortable. I had a wild impulse to start hassling him, maybe
even break another window. As if in answer to this idea, a
state trooper car pulled into the parking lot and parked ri;ht
next to my Chrysler Grand Fury.

"Okay," I said to Louise, "I'll have a hot dog and some
ice cream."

She frowned. "What kind of ice cream?"

"Dutch Almond Mocha."

She stifled a laugh. Papakakis turned around and

pointed to the wall where the menu was. "Chocolate, vanilla, or strawberry, sir."

"Oh, right, I forgot." I smiled at Louise. "I'll tell you what. Forget the hot dog, forget the ice cream. I'll just have a cup of coffee."

When she left to get the coffee I spoke to Papakakis. "How's business?"

He looked at me briefly, turned back to his work and said, "Not bad." And then after a silence, he said, "I haven't seen you before. You live around here?"

"No, but I used to. When I was in high school I used to hang out here, in your parking lot."

He grunted and said, "Yeah, that stuff is history now. Friday and Saturday nights I got security people here. I'm happy to spend the money. I put up with enough grief over the years. I'm too old for that shit now."

I laughed. "You look like you're holding up pretty well." And then, entirely on impulse, I asked, "You got kids?"

He turned around and looked at me. His expression was at first suspicious, but when he saw that mine was sincere, his face relaxed and he smiled. "Do I got kids?" he asked rhetorically. "I got eleven grandchildren, for Chrissakes."

"Eleven?"

"Hold on, let me show you." He marched toward the back and disappeared through some swinging doors. That left me to wonder what the cops found so interesting about my car. They were standing in front of it, looking at it, and talking to each other. But it all looked pretty casual. Probably a conversation about horsepower.

Papakakis strode out of the kitchen with a leather-bound photo album. I looked through it, making the occasional polite comment, which wasn't difficult because his grandchildren were all really nice-looking. When I was done

I handed the album back to him. "You're a lucky man," I said.

He looked at me with a good deal more interest now. "So," he said, "you used to make trouble in my parking lot. What are you doing now?"

"I'm a lawyer," I said, just to keep it short.

He raised his eyebrows, impressed. "That's a good field—law."

"Yeah," I said, "it's really good."

He went back to his work, and when I turned and glanced again at the cops I saw something I didn't want to see. One of them was back in his own car with the door open and the inside light on. He looked like he was talking into the receiver of a two-way radio.

A chill ran through me as I sipped my coffee and stared hard at the orange formica counter. The hum from the overhead lights, which I hadn't previously even noticed, now came to me in a roar. At the same moment that I heard the door open and saw the blue uniforms out of the corner of my eye, Papakakis asked, "What kind of law you do?"

The cops walked right by me, bullshitting about something or other, and settled at the counter across the room. I exhaled and looked at Papakakis. "Probate."

Papakakis smiled knowingly. "That's where the money is—huh?"

"Yeah." I raised my voice and asked, "Hey, Louise, how 'bout another cup of coffee?" To Papakakis I said, "I have a confession."

He looked at me good-naturedly.

"About twelve years or so ago I broke your window." I gestured toward the front door. "That one."

He put his rag down and straightened his body. His eyes glazed over as he searched his memory. "You threw a rock?"

I nodded.

"I grabbed you?"

I shook my head in wonder. "I can't believe you remember."

He shrugged ironically. "In twenty years it's only happened twice. That one set me back eight hundred bucks."

"Oh, come on," I said, "your insurance paid for it."

He shook his head sadly. "I was tight for cash at the time and I let the policy lapse for a month. It was the last day of that month that you broke the fucking window. I tried to sneak it in but they laughed at me. I had to eat the whole eight hundred."

"Oh, man," I said, "I feel terrible."

"Don't be ridiculous," he said, almost sternly. "It's in the past. I'm selling this place at the end of the year, I'm moving to Arizona near two of my daughters. I'm fine."

I nodded soberly. "That's great." One of the cops, a dark-featured guy with a long skinny nose, seemed to be giving me a lot of attention, but somehow it didn't bother me. I was too happy to be talking to Papakakis.

"You taught me a great lesson that night," I said to him.

He took a deep breath. "I roughed you up a little bit, didn't I? I'm sorry."

"No no," I replied quickly. "You taught me a great lesson. You taught me fear."

He stared at me for a long moment. "Is that such a great lesson?"

"Oh, yeah, I think so. Without fear you have no civilization."

He looked a little confused so I started to explain my point, using my hands for emphasis. "It's like, primitive man, right, like the caveman, he took what he wanted when he wanted it. He'd kill another man for food, for woman, for shelter, what have you. Now we have all these laws and we have all these ideas like 'respect for others,' like 'respect for personal property.' I mean, I can remember on my report card in elementary school there was a whole section called something like that and you actually got graded. But it's all sentiment, it's all bullshit and hypocrisy because it's all based on fear, fear of reprisal. We're just as greedy and unprincipled as we always were. We're just sneakier now."

"Right," said Papakakis. "We got lawyers now."

He took his rag back in hand and was sort of half looking at me and half cleaning his machine. "You know," he said, "my lawyer's a young guy about your age. Much different kind of guy though."

"Listen," I said, "I didn't mean to give you a whole speech. I'm in a weird mood, and being here brings back a lot of memories."

"Hey," he said, "you can talk all you want." His face flushed in embarrassment, and he turned away from me. "It's interesting. It's very interesting."

"I'd love to," I said, standing up and throwing a dollar down on the counter. "But I gotta run. My name's Eddie Black."

"George Papakakis," he said, giving me a nearly debilitating handshake.

I wished him luck in Arizona, he wished me luck in probate law, and I left.

I was back on the thruway for less than a mile when the state troopers appeared in my rear-view mirror. My whole body turned instantly cold, and when they pulled close and put the flashers on, my insides started to riot. I might have even lost consciousness for a second because the next thing I saw was this cop from the Dairy Maid walking toward me. Both vehicles were on the shoulder of the highway. I lowered my window a few inches and stared at the steering wheel.

"I'm really sorry I had to pull you over like that," he said.

I slowly raised my head to look at him. Up close, and despite the mustache, he looked about seventeen years old.

"I'm Ralph Fortunato. You went out with my sister Linda in tenth grade. I thought it was you back there, but I just couldn't believe it. But when I asked George your name I had to talk to you. We watch your show a lot, I mean mainly Linda does, and you know she always brags about how she went out with you and how she broke it up because you were too grabby."

I ran my hand over my face. I felt as if I was emerging from a deep thaw. Linda Fortunato: a nice girl with a locally famous body. Why had she never let me touch it?

"How is Linda?"

Ralph nodded vigorously. "She's good. She's married, got a coupl'a kids. I'll tell ya, she'd flip if I got some kind of personal autograph type thing."

He handed me a clipboard and a pen. I wrote: TO LINDA FORTUNATO, THE FINEST WOMAN I HAVE EVER KNOWN. AND THE MOST HONORABLE. I signed and handed it back to Ralph.

He read it and scrunched his face in delight. "That's perfect! She'll go ape-shit!" Then he looked at me seriously and said, "I think I scared you a little bit. I'm really sorry. Probably made you feel like some kind of criminal."

"It's okay," I said softly. "Maybe I have a guilty conscience."

"Na," said Ralph, "it's always the innocent people, the ones who never did anything wrong in their life that get scared when you pull them over."

I looked at him soberly. "Is that right?"

He nodded professionally. "Believe me."

22

Jennifer trained her pretty blue eyes on me and said, "What do you think of the picture?"

"It stinks."

She grinned. "You're good, though. Dick is telling everyone how terrific you are."

I gestured with my hand as if to dismiss the idea. "Dick is always telling someone how terrific they are. I haven't heard that word as much in my whole life as I have in the last six weeks. Everything and everyone out here is fucking terrific."

"Is your fucking terrific?" asked Jennifer.

I laughed shortly, shook my head, and turned away. It happened to be a good question because despite the heightened exposure my career had recently given me, the last woman I had been terrifically intimate with had been Charlotte, and that was over a year ago. In that time my continuing role on "Hillsdale" had made me mildly famous. I appeared, along with two other male soap stars, on the cover of *People* magazine, and if I'd given one interview in the last several months I'd given fifty.

Now I was in San Francisco on leave from the show and doing a movie for Paramount Pictures. It was a sort of romantic comedy triangle with me as the "other man." I'd gone over the script several times and still couldn't believe anyone could get money for such a ridiculous story, but my role was, I thought, the best in the picture. I had a couple of genuinely funny scenes and a minimum of painful lines.

I smiled and half listened as Jennifer related a nasty little anecdote about the female lead in the movie. Jennifer was what they called a production assistant, though even after six weeks I couldn't tell you what she did, except that her father was the producer. She was young, maybe twenty, bright and bouncy, and we had spontaneously flirted with each other since the beginning of the picture. Things would have been consummated by now, but I had evaded and avoided, telling myself it was bad business, but really just being scared to get close to her until tonight, when I had asked her to come back to the hotel with me.

The waitress came with the next round of drinks—Jack Daniels for me and a Diet Coke for Jennifer. I was pleasantly buzzed, and I moved my chair next to Jennifer's and kissed her below the ear. She smiled happily and put her hand on my thigh.

"Excuse me." A stout middle-aged woman dressed in bright polyester was standing nervously at our table. "Are you Eddie Black?" she asked.

"He's recognized everywhere," whispered Jennifer dramatically, at the same time moving her hand around in my lap.

"Yes, ma'am," I said to the woman.

"Would you mind very much," she said, taking a pen and paper from her purse. "I don't do this sort of thing, but it's for my husband over there." She pointed to a man two tables away. He wore a colorful Hawaiian shirt, and he had his back to us. "He's too embarrassed to come over."

"Oh, don't worry," giggled Jennifer. "He loves giving autographs." I took the pen in hand. "What is your husband's name?"

"Nathan."

To Nathan, I began . . .

"Nathan Greenberg. I'm Ruth Greenberg."

The paper, the glasses, the whole table in front of my eyes seemed suddenly far away. The blood rushed to my head, and my chest began to pound. I didn't want to do it, but my head turned on its own and I found myself looking into the deeply tanned, perpetually smiling face of Nate Greenberg.

"Small world, isn't it?" he said.

I nodded soberly, and his own face became more serious. "How are things, Eddie?"

"Things are okay," I replied. "How about you?"

He shrugged contentedly. "Can't complain. Just got back from Hawaii—fuckin' heaven on earth."

"Heaven on earth," I said thoughtfully.

"Yeah," he said. "I figure I better find my heavens now because you never know which way you're going when you die. Know what I mean?"

I laughed. "Yeah, I know what you mean."

"Speaking of heaven," he continued, "I read about Willie. You go to the funeral?"

I nodded.

Greenberg leaned forward. "Any big names there?"

"Oh yeah," I said. "Al Capone was standing right next to me."

He laughed heartily. "Anyway," he said, "it's nice to die in your sleep."

I scribbled my name on the piece of paper and handed it to Mrs. Greenberg. "Nice meeting you."

She was confused, looking back and forth between me and her husband, but she thanked me warmly and apologized for disturbing us.

When the Greenbergs left a few minutes later, Jennifer asked, "Who was that guy?"

"Someone I knew in New York."

"You turned white as a sheet when you looked at him," she said, and then added in a mild pout, "and you got soft in about half a second."

"Sorry."

"He was weird," she continued. "Looked like an appliance salesman or something. And his frumpy wife—God."

"Jennifer," I said sharply, "you should learn to be more tolerant."

"What do you mean?"

"I mean not everybody grew up in Bel Air with fancy-ass movie people running around. Some people sell appliances, and their wives get frumpy."

She crinkled her nose and scrunched down in her chair, a childishness that made me feel uncomfortably old.

"Oh, Eddie," she breathed, batting her eyes in a put-on sort of wickedness, "teach me more."

Though Jennifer was young, she showed a maturity beyond her years. As I lay next to her staring at the ceiling she stroked my chest and said, "Don't feel bad about it, Eddie. I don't want you to. I want to try it again whenever you're ready."

I turned to her and kissed her on the forehead. Then I got up from the bed and started to put my clothes on. She flicked on the bedside light and sat up.

"Where are you going?"

"I'm going to go down and have a drink. Go to sleep, I'll be okay."

She made a low whining sound and said, "I wanted to sleep next to you."

I looked at her small, perfect breasts, appreciating them the way I would a piece of artwork in a museum. I walked over to her and kissed each of them tenderly.

She murmured and said, "Come back to bed. I'm gonna take care of you."

I shook my head and continued buttoning my shirt. "I need some air. I need a drink."

It was just after one when I got up to the bar. There wasn't much going on: a group of Japanese businessmen at one of the tables and just a smattering of other people, mostly young couples. I took a small table at the back near the window, looking out at the buildings of the financial district and the bridge to Oakland, the lights of which illuminated the water of the bay. It was a majestic view, and it lifted my spirits some to gaze at it, but I still must have looked about how I felt because the barmaid treated me with a sympathy that was palpable, as if I was a quadriplegic or something.

I was in the middle of my second scotch when Greenberg arrived, or rather burst on the scene, accompanied by two emaciated-looking black whores. He was still wearing the Hawaiian shirt, and I supposed I hadn't noticed the bright yellow pants before. They were settled at the bar, the women on chairs and Greenberg leaning over between them in a boyish pose, his big ass protruding, and appearing from a distance as some strange tropical growth. Though they were at least thirty feet away from me I clearly heard Greenberg order three Mai Tais and "plenty of nuts."

I briefly considered leaving, but I doubted I could make my exit without him seeing me. Also, there was something about his presence that was compelling, and it gave me an idea. When I ordered my next round I asked the barmaid to buy the man in the colorful shirt a Mai Tai on me.

I watched her give him the drink and saw him turn abruptly to face me. Without a word to his company he picked up his drink and made his way in my direction. He sat down heavily and took a pack of Camels out of his shirt pocket. He lighted one and exhaled, bathing me in a torrent of smoke and alcohol fumes.

"You're looking at a man," he said, "who just spent three hundred dollars for a piece of ass. Correction: two pieces of ass." He chuckled. "I thought I was gonna die, but I figured it was worth it."

I smiled softly. "Whatever makes you happy, Nate."

He grunted and eyed me shrewdly. "Me happy? It's you that's got it made. You're young, you're successful, and you're free—thanks to me." He giggled. "It rhymes, it's poetry."

"What does it benefit a man," I said, "to gain the whole world and lose his soul? That's poetry."

"That ain't poetry, it's bullshit."

I shrugged and looked out the window.

"You got complaints, Eddie? Is that what that's supposed to mean? Why aren't you downstairs humping that sweet high-school ass I saw you with? Enjoy life, for Chrissakes. If there's one thing I can tell you after fifty-seven years on this earth it's to enjoy life. Every minute, every day."

"That doesn't work for everybody."

"Why not?" he demanded.

"I don't know," I said easily, "maybe there's a moral aspect to things."

"Ha ha ha," he said sarcastically, hitting me three times with his hot breath. "Look who's talking about moral aspects to things." He paused to give me a sharp look. "And this late in the day."

I nodded. "I've changed, Nate. I'm a different man."

He lifted his drink. "Good for you. To the new and different Eddie Black—the one with the moral aspect."

I raised my own glass and touched his. Then I looked him straight in the eye and said, "I'm turning myself in."

He frowned slightly and sipped his drink. The statement hadn't registered. "Turning yourself in for what?"

"For killing Frank Popowski."

His eyes widened and focused sharply on mine. "That's a very bad joke."

"It's no joke. The party's over."

Even in the dim light I could see some of the color leave his face, and his mouth hung open slightly. I felt myself warming to the role.

"Doesn't make any sense," he said, shaking his head.

I looked down at the table and spoke in a very low voice. "It does to me. It's the only way."

"What the fuck are you talking about?" he demanded, his voice cracking on the last word and sending it up to the ceiling.

I looked at him calmly. "Someone's gotta answer for Frank, and for Vincent."

He swallowed hard and moved his lips against each other awkwardly, like an old man with no teeth. "You're smart," he said. "Why are you talking so stupid?"

I smiled sadly. "Sometimes you have to have the wisdom to be stupid, not smart."

He leaned back and looked at me sickly. "You're out of your mind."

I nodded. "That's right. I'm out of my mind." I leaned forward and put my hand on his fat, hairy, sweaty arm. "I'm

glad we ran into each other. This way you'll have advance notice. You can make plans—move to Brazil or something."

"I can't move to Brazil," he whispered fiercely. "You
can't do this to me."

I continued in a matter-of-fact tone. "When this thing
busts, it's going to bust big. I mean because of Willie and
all . . ."

He moaned softly and put his head in his hands. I was
feeling stabs of pleasure, seemingly in direct proportion to
his pain.

He looked up suddenly. "Why are you doing this?"

"Because it stinks," I whispered. "I stink, you stink, the
whole thing stinks, and I can smell it every minute of every
day."

He breathed heavily and stared past me out the window.
Then his eyes went back to mine, and he said, "Can I ask you
a personal question?"

"Sure."

"When was the last time you went to synagogue?"

I hesitated before answering. "I can't remember."

His eyes lit up in excitement, and he nodded knowingly.
"Go to synagogue. I'm not kidding, Eddie." His mouth was
twitching. "I go every Saturday. I even went in Hawaii. The
comfort you get, the comfort you get when you have a problem—it's tremendous." He patted my arm and leaned closer.
I could see and smell the perspiration on his face. "That's
your problem, don't you see? You have all this success, all
this youth, you're good-looking—you're a beautiful boy, yet
you're unhappy. Why? Not because of Frank Popowski, not
because of Vincent Woppo. I'll tell you why—you don't have
God in your life, you don't have religion."

I leaned back in my chair and nodded thoughtfully. He
took this as a sign of hope, and his eyes fixed on mine more

sharply. "The bitch of it is that you're already part of the greatest religious heritage there ever was." He paused for drama. "You're a Jew."

I put my hand over my face and took a deep and troubled breath.

Greenberg grabbed the glasses and stood up. His chest was heaving, and the sweat was now pouring down his face and neck. "I'm gonna get us another round because I'm gonna talk to you more about this. I'm no intellectual, Eddie, I never claimed to be, but I been around longer than you, and I know what's important in life. And it's got nothing to do with money or fame." He made an expansive gesture with his arm to include the bar and the hotel. "Or any of this shit. What are you drinking?"

"Bourbon."

As I watched him waddle quickly toward the bar I wondered how much longer to play this out. I decided that when he returned I'd tell him I was only fucking around and we'd enjoy a drink together. He's not such a bad guy, I thought, the pudgy bastard.

He was making his way back now, but as he stepped down the two little stairs to our section of the bar something fell out of his shirt pocket; it was his cigarettes. He stood there uncertainly for a second, frowning, but when I started to get up to help him he ordered me to sit down. He put my bourbon down on a chair and squatted awkwardly to pick up the cigarettes. But then something went wrong. His body went rigid for a split second, his head popped up straight, and an absolutely inhuman sound came out of him. His right arm swung wide, sending the Mai Tai flying five or six feet across the room. He managed to grab onto the little bannister next to the stairs and raise himself halfway up, but then he bellowed again and collapsed in a heap on the floor.

I sat in my chair, paralyzed, and it was as if in a dream that I saw the few remaining people in the bar rush toward him. A woman screamed, someone yelled for a doctor, and another woman was kneeling beside Greenberg and pounding his chest.

I finally managed to get up and over there. I knew Greenberg was dead before I looked at him because I had seen the light go out of his eyes, and I had seen the unequivocal way in which his body had descended to the floor. The woman who'd been trying to revive him had already given up and was looking around helplessly. I could read no attitude or emotion in Greenberg's face. He looked neither relaxed nor troubled. He was simply gone. I walked slowly around the people, down an aisle at the side of the room, and then I too was gone.

I slipped in bed beside Jennifer. She was lying on her side, her back to me, and I settled in against her, seeking just a little warmth, a little comfort. But my body came instantly alive, and I started to stroke her and move against her. She responded, but slowly and sleepily, so I turned her on her back and kissed and licked the length of her. Soon she was coming back at me, matching my hunger, and the heat from our bodies was nearly suffocating. Then she started to scratch and bite, and when she tried to roll me over and get on top I sensed the vaguest hint of a peformance so I pinned her arms against the bed and took her the way I wanted to.

And then we lay on our backs, side by side, our chests heaving in unison.

"That was a good idea," said Jennifer.

"What was?"

"To go down and get a drink, to get some air."

I turned to see her smiling at me, and for a moment I was able to smile back, but then my eyes dropped, my stomach and chest became tight, and I felt vividly the sensation of being forcibly ripped apart from her and the room. It was with a feeling of desperation that I embraced Jennifer, my head in her breast, squeezing and moving against her as if looking for a hole large enough to crawl inside and disappear. She put her arms on my shoulder, but limply, and a moment later when I sensed her discomfort I pulled away and moved to my own side of the bed.

23

It was my first Sunday back in New York, and amidst a carnival of kids and kites and fathers and ball-players, I stood on the Great Lawn in Central Park and pitched a wiffle ball toward Benjamin. No matter how many times I told him he wouldn't hold his hands properly around the bat, but he had somehow understood the idea of keeping his eye on the ball, and, as a result, he was hitting some pretty mean shots. Every time he made solid contact he squealed, chased down the ball, and fell on it as if recovering a fumble in football.

We kept playing and playing, not talking much, but establishing a rhythm with the ball and the bat and our laughter. It was the sort of game I used to tire of easily but after three months in California, our longest separation ever, his presence was hitting a strange sentimental spot in me that I didn't think I still had.

His best hit of the day was a screaming line drive that whistled past my ear. As I turned to watch him chase the ball I saw Laura walking down a path toward us. She was wearing jeans, a bulky blue sweater, and carrying the Sunday paper.

She waved to us and then sat down on the grass while
we kept playing. Soon we were joined by a fat Chinese kid, a
little older than Benjamin, and soon after that I was able to
withdraw from the game and take a seat next to Laura.

"He's really happy to see you," she said. "I haven't seen
him this excited in ages."

I took a deep breath and said, "Yeah." Then I stretched
out on my back and closed my eyes to the sun. For a few moments Laura tried to make small talk, but I was too distracted
and distrustful of my own voice, so I answered her only in
grunts and monosyllables.

Finally I sat up. In looking around at all the people in
the park I felt desperately out of things. I glanced at Laura,
who was now buried in the magazine section of the paper,
and I thought: Let's remarry, have another kid or two, and
move to Scarsdale.

She might as well have heard me because she suddenly
emerged from her paper and looked at me with a clinical sort
of interest. "Are you okay, Eddie?"

"I don't know," I said. "I'm feeling a little nauseous."

"What did you have for breakfast?"

"I don't remember."

Benjamin and the Chinese kid were already starting to
argue. It looked as if the other kid wanted to take a few
swings and Benjamin didn't want to hear about it. I yelled to
him to let the kid hit, and when he started to come over to
"explain" the whole thing to me I pointed sternly from the
bat to the other boy. They traded places and continued playing.

I smiled at Laura. "The boy needs a firm hand once in a
while."

"Yeah," she said drily, "it's easy to apply a firm hand
once a week." Then she touched my arm quickly and said,
"I'm sorry, that wasn't fair."

"Yes it was," I replied. "It was more than fair."

"You're a good father, Eddie. Whatever else you are, you're a good father."

"What do you mean, 'whatever else I am'? What else am I?"

She looked at me speculatively. "I don't know," she began. "You seem sad. You've seemed sad for a while now. I don't know what it's about, I just hope you're okay."

I turned away, my face burning. I had the impulse to snap at her, but it passed. "I've had some hard times, Laura, some very hard times." I stopped, angry at myself, and shook my head. "That's not it at all. The fact is I've done some bad things—to people, to other people. It wasn't intentional, but . . ."

She put her hand on my arm to stop me. "Don't hold on to that stuff, Eddie. People are resilient, they bounce back."

A hopeless and ironic laugh escaped my lips. "Not always," I said quietly. "They don't always bounce back."

"Do you want to talk about it?"

I took her hand off my arm and put it to my lips. I kissed it and then stood up. "I've really gotta go. Next Sunday?"

In looking up at me she shaded her eyes with her hand, a very attractive gesture. "Next Sunday's great."

I walked over to Benjamin to say goodbye. He leaped into my arms, and I smelled his sweat and felt the beating of his heart against my chest. He put his arms around my neck and I squeezed him a little tighter, trying to hold the moment.

24

"**Y**ou don't look too well," I said to Suzanne. "Would you like a drink?"

She sat on the couch and shook her head. "I've been sad lately. I've been thinking about Emily."

I walked over and sat next to her on the couch. "You'll get over it, honey. Life goes on."

"I know," she replied, "but I've been having nightmares about her. If I only knew who killed her, and why, then maybe I could learn to live with it."

I felt a wave of disgust pass through me, and I shook my head and turned away from her.

Larry's voice bombarded across the set. "Cut! Cut!" He appeared in front of the stage and glowered at me. "What the hell is your problem?" he asked.

I stood up from the couch and walked toward him. "How much longer are we going to play this out?" I asked heatedly.

"What are you talking about?"

"I'm talking about the fucking character. He killed her sister, for Chrissakes. They're married, they're supposed to be in love, and he killed her sister. I don't think it's right."

"So now you're a thinker," said Larry. "All this time I thought you were an actor."

"I can't do it anymore," I said, shaking my head. "This is not a character, this is a tin man. Every time the murder is mentioned he grimaces, he looks at the wall; phony, phony, phony."

Larry pointed a finger at me. "I don't go for this temperamental actor shit. I'm warning you."

Our eyes locked for several seconds. "He's gotta confess, Larry. At least to her, he's gotta confess."

"You know the Greyhound slogan?" asked Larry with irritation. He gestured off stage toward Steve, a bearded guy of about my own age, who was the head writer. "Leave the driving to us."

I shook my head in exasperation and looked at Steve. "It's no good," I said forcefully. "I'm losing my feeling for it because I'm not playing a part, I'm playing a stick. And I'm tired of it."

"Get another fucking job!" yelled Larry. His face had colored deeply, and for a second I thought he was going to come up on stage after me. Steve came over quickly and stood between us, facing me.

"Eddie," he said calmly, "a confession wouldn't be in character for Stone. It wouldn't be in his best interest."

"Screw his best interest! We've had enough of him acting in his best interest." I walked to the edge of the stage and lowered my voice. "He lost his head when he killed Emily. And she had a knife. He's basically a decent guy—we've gotta give him a chance to prove it."

Steve and Larry were looking up at me, and just for an instant they struck me as two little puppy dogs, awaiting direction.

"I've got the whole scene in my head. Let me try it."

I thought I had them, but then a cloud passed over Larry's face. "Get another job," he said. "Go back to that meat truck."

I gave him a hard look. "That's not funny."

Steve was scratching his beard and frowning. "What happens when he confesses? What does she do?"

"There's lots of possibilities," I said excitedly. "He could actually go to the police, they could go together. She would stand behind him because she knows he's not really a killer—she knows the real man and she loves him."

"I don't know," said Steve worriedly.

"Oh, come on," I said, and I sensed with distaste the note of pleading in my voice. "The way it is now it's a sick, fucked-up relationship. I mean, the guy is just a rich, satisfied, complacent, arrogant . . ."

"Like you," said Larry.

I pointed a finger at him as I felt the heat flood my face. "Don't you ever say that to me," I said menacingly. "I am not satisfied! I am not complacent!" I stood there for a moment, breathing heavily. When I managed to tear my eyes off of Larry's face I saw that everyone on the set was looking at me. They all seemed to have the same oddly curious expression on their faces. I had the impulse to flee to my dressing room, but my feet were nailed to the stage. I closed my eyes for a second and tried to gather myself.

"Listen," I said, "let me try it. Suzanne doesn't have to say anything. We can pick it up from the last line. Let me just give it a shot."

Steve took a deep breath and looked at Larry. "I'd like to see it. What do you say?"

"Sure," said Larry. His voice was calm and subdued, but his eyes bored into me and betrayed a deep resentment.

I walked back to the couch and sat down. "Are you ready, Kathy?"

She nodded quickly and smiled. "I like it."

"I know," said Suzanne, "but I've been having nightmares about her. If I only knew who killed her, and why, then maybe I could learn to live with it."

I took her hand and kissed it. "It's time you knew the truth, Suzanne. You may never want to see me again, but you have to know." I paused and moved closer to her. "Emily was against us from the start, you know that. She kept pounding and pounding on me, saying I didn't love you, saying I only wanted your father's money: all lies. She came to my office that day, but she pulled a knife on me. I told her to leave, but she wouldn't listen, she kept coming closer to me with the knife and . . ." I stopped again, choked with emotion. "When I saw the letter opener on the desk I started to lose my own mind. I should have kept talking, I should have run away, but I couldn't think, I couldn't even breathe. All I saw was her trying to destroy me, to destroy us, and I was scared. I was so scared." I paused one last time, closed my eyes for a second, and then looked at her squarely. "Suzanne, it was me that killed Emily."

I heard Larry's voice end the scene, and Kathy leaned over and kissed me on the forehead. "Eddie, that was great."

I walked quickly off stage to my dressing room. Once inside, I sat at the table and wept quietly for several minutes. Finally, I started to get it together. I blew my nose a couple of times and then washed my face in the sink. It was only then that I heard the soft tapping at my door and realized it had been going on for at least a few minutes.

"Come in," I said.

Larry opened the door slowly and looked at me. "You okay?" he asked.

I walked over to him. "I'm sorry, Larry. I'm really sorry."

He was stiff at first, but then patted me on the arm and smiled. "Don't be sorry. You showed a lot of balls, and the scene was strong, very strong." He gestured outside. "Steve is running around like a chicken with its head cut off. He's gonna write a whole series of shows off this." Larry spread his hands to suggest limitless possibilities.

He sat down in a chair and I sat down, too. "I appreciate you letting me run with it like that."

"Appreciate it?" he asked ironically. "I thought you were gonna kill me."

I took a deep breath. "It was important to me."

He nodded soberly. "I could see that. I was wondering where it all came from."

I looked at him openly, but I didn't say anything.

"I kept thinking back to that other shot," he continued, "the one where you had to kill Emily. You fainted, blacked out completely."

"I remember." My eyes went past his head and settled on the wall for a second. Then I looked back at him. "I really don't like violence."

He nodded and stood up from the chair. "Anyway, I'm glad you did it." He laughed. "I'm glad you got it off your chest." Still smiling, he pointed a finger at me. "Don't forget, I'm still the boss here. I was putting shows on the air when you were in diapers."

I stood up, we shook hands, and he left.

It was more than two weeks later, on a Sunday night, that I pulled the car into the parking garage and gave it over to the attendant. I smiled at John, the man who was in charge of the garage. He was a huge West Indian, a good-natured vigorous man of about fifty.

"Nice weekend, Mr. Black?"

"Yeah," I said, "very nice."

"You look good," he boomed. "You look like you had some good loving."

I laughed and opened the door to get to the elevator.

"I saw the show on Friday," he said to me.

"Oh yeah? What did you think?"

"Took a lot of guts to tell her," he said, shaking his head. "I didn't know the guy had that much heart."

I let the door slip closed. "You like him better now, huh?"

He looked at me oddly.

"I mean, he's a better man now, right?"

"Depends," said John reluctantly, "it all depends. True repentance is between a man and his God. I have yet to see that on 'Hillsdale.' "

I nodded and opened the door again. "We'll have to work it into the script."

He laughed heartily, and I could hear the richness of his voice all the way to the elevator.

When I got upstairs I lay down in bed, lighted a cigarette, and turned on the answering machine. After absently listening to three or four messages, the whole of my attention was captured by one sentence.

"This is Detective Parker of the New York City Police Department."

I sat up immediately and stopped the machine. I pressed the rewind button and started it again, but the words hadn't changed.

"This is Detective Parker of the New York City Police Department. You might not remember me, but we met during the Frank Popowski murder investigation. I was Detective Greenberg's partner." There was a pause, and then he continued. "The case has never been officially closed and there are some, uh, inconsistencies that I need to clear up." There was another break while he cleared his throat. "You're one of the few people still around, and I have a feeling you can help me. My telephone number is 828-1000—that's evening hours. During the day I sit around and watch soap operas."

I sat on the edge of the bed without moving. When the cigarette had burned down I let it burn my fingers for a few seconds and then I tossed it on the floor. Some amount of time passed; it could have been twenty minutes, it could have been an hour and a half. I replayed the end of the tape and then picked up the telephone and dialed the number. After three rings the receiver was picked up and the voice said, "Parker."

I was struck by the simplicity of his greeting. We would keep it simple this time.

"Eddie Black."